Praise for the novels of Valerie Frankel

"You'll go gaga for this kooky romantic comedy about finding The One in the most unlikely of places." — *Cosmopolitan*

"Glib and funny, Frankel's always wickedly entertaining." —*People*

"Laugh-out-loud funny. . . . [It's] impossible not to root for Frankel's plucky, determined heroine." —*Booklist*

"Amusing farce, with pearls of urban wisdom and some great zingers." —*Kirkus Reviews*

"Frankel's wit and playfulness make the tale scroll right along." —*Publishers Weekly*

"Charming and highly entertaining. A must read for anyone who has a sister." —Candace Bushnell, author of *Sex and the City*

"Valerie Frankel has created a well-written, true-to-life story that will keep you interested until the end." —Romance Reviews Today

"An interesting character study . . . a fine relationship tale that showcases love hurts, but anything less is loneliness."
—The Best Reviews

"You won't be able to help yourself from rooting for Adora during her bloodless revolution, just as you won't be able to stop yourself from feeling her heartbreak along the way. This is definitely a read that's well worth your time!" —Teens Read Too

"Even the pickiest readers won't be disappointed! Valerie Frankel creates original, interesting characters and sticks them in the equally original, funny, and entertaining story she tells."
—The Edge of the Forest

"*Fringe Girl in Love* definitely read up to expectation and provided me with a *fantastic* laugh. Every chapter kept you on your toes, and I often caught myself smiling and laughing out loud. *Great read!*"
—Flamingnet

Fringe Benefits

Valerie Frankel

nal
JaM
books

NAL Jam
Published by New American Library, a division of
Penguin Group (USA) Inc., 375 Hudson Street,
New York, New York 10014, USA
Penguin Group (Canada), 90 Eglinton Avenue East, Suite 700, Toronto,
Ontario M4P 2Y3, Canada (a division of Pearson Penguin Canada Inc.)
Penguin Books Ltd., 80 Strand, London WC2R 0RL, England
Penguin Ireland, 25 St. Stephen's Green, Dublin 2,
Ireland (a division of Penguin Books Ltd.)
Penguin Group (Australia), 250 Camberwell Road, Camberwell, Victoria 3124,
Australia (a division of Pearson Australia Group Pty. Ltd.)
Penguin Books India Pvt. Ltd., 11 Community Centre, Panchsheel Park,
New Delhi—110 017, India
Penguin Group (NZ), 67 Apollo Drive, Rosedale, North Shore 0632,
New Zealand (a division of Pearson New Zealand Ltd.)
Penguin Books (South Africa) (Pty.) Ltd., 24 Sturdee Avenue,
Rosebank, Johannesburg 2196, South Africa

Penguin Books Ltd., Registered Offices:
80 Strand, London WC2R 0RL, England

First published by NAL Jam, an imprint of New American Library,
a division of Penguin Group (USA) Inc.

First Printing, September 2008
1 3 5 7 9 10 8 6 4 2

Copyright © Valerie Frankel, 2008
All rights reserved

NAL JAM and logo are trademarks of Penguin Group (USA) Inc.

LIBRARY OF CONGRESS CATALOGING-IN-PUBLICATION DATA:
Frankel, Valerie.
Fringe benefits / Valerie Frankel.
p. cm.
Summary: Instead of the European vacations and sleepaway camps of summers past,
Dora finds herself stuck in Brooklyn after her junior year at Brownstone Collegiate
Institute, waitressing at an exclusive tennis and squash club where
new responsibilities and exciting relationships abound.
ISBN: 978-0-451-22496-5
[1. Interpersonal relations—Fiction. 2. Responsibility—Fiction. 3. Summer—Fiction.
4. Work—Fiction. 5. Brooklyn (New York, N.Y.)—Fiction.] I. Title.
PZ7.F8553Fj 2008
[Fic]—dc22   008009399

Set in New Caledonia
Designed by Alissa Amell

Printed in the United States of America

Fringe Benefits

1

"Rising." The word had such grandiose implications. I loved the sound of it, the taste of it on my tongue. As of five minutes ago, I was, officially, a Rising Senior. A person on the ascent. I closed my eyes and pictured myself rising off the ground, lifting like a balloon over the Brownstone Collegiate Institute, looking down at my school, smiling with nostalgic beauty as a melancholic tear slid off my pink cheek. I watched the salty globule descend and come to a splat on the threshold, only a moment before the doors burst open and scores of frenetic kids ran out onto the street for summer break.

Soon, I would cross that threshold, and get Out of Here for the next thirteen weeks. Grinning with relief, I—I being me, Adora Benet—slammed my locker good and closed.

"Another year over," I said to my two best friends, Eli Stomp and Liza Greene. They were waiting for me, their backs against the row of lockers. All told, junior year had been a toughie, but I'd survived with my social and academic standing (such as it was) intact.

"Maybe we should sing the opening number to *High School Musical 2*," said Liza, whose shining blue eyes, silken blond hair and eager expression make her the human equivalent of melted butter in a glass bowl.

"One note, and I *will* kill you," said Eli.

"Empty threat," I said. "You'd maim and dismember, sure. But you draw the line at murder."

"In this case, I'd be justified," said Eli. She looked like a China doll, as always, in a red tank and denim mini, her stick-straight black hair streaming down her back. She was midnight to Liza's high noon. I'd say Eli was yin to Liza's yang, but she might interpret that as racially loaded.

Liza asked, "What's our first stop as free citizens? Grind?"

Grind was our joint, a café on Montague Street that served cakes, cookies, and all manner of caffeinated beverages. Eli's boyfriend, Charlie, was a barista there. I was completely in favor of this relationship. Charlie was a devoted boyfriend, for one thing. He made Eli as happy as I'd ever seen her—and I'd seen a lot of her, having lived on consecutive floors of the same brownstone building, along with Liza, since Eli's parents brought her to Brooklyn from China when she was two. Our families had all moved up and out of that building since, but we three were still thisclose. Perhaps the greatest thing about Eli and Charlie's love: He got us free fraps, lats and lemon cakes at Grind, which had upped my caffeine consumption to teeth-chattering levels.

Eli said, "Warning. Charlie's not working, so we'll have to pay."

Liza and I gasped and clutched each other for support.

"You used to pay for coffee every day," said Eli.

"But I've grown accustomed to a certain standard of living," I said. "I'm not sure I can go back."

"You might have to. Charlie's going to quit Grind," said Eli.

Reeling backward, I blurted, "Don't say it like that! You have to deliver the bad news gently. Ease into it. First say, 'Charlie's cutting back on his hours.' Let me get used to that, and then lower the boom."

Liza said, "Can we just go? I'm *starving*."

We went. The walk took only a few minutes, but it felt like forever. My backpack was twice its usual size, stuffed with the detritus of a year, including a pair of beloved yoga pants that had been wedged into the dark, dank corner of my locker. When I couldn't find them anywhere at home, I'd accused Mom of throwing them away. We'd had a big fight about it. Oops.

It was a relief to drop the bundle on the floor when we finally got to Grind. My shoulders were not strong like bull. They were weak like meerkat. Maybe I should put "build muscle mass" on my summer to-do list. Beef up, pump iron. Go jogging with Dad.

Riiiight. I might as well learn Farsi, too, while I was at it.

Once we'd secured our drinks—Liza also got a ham and cheese croissant—we three best pals, practically from birth, sat down to bask in our collective joy and freedom. Nothing but fun in the city to come for the next three months. I'd fled Brooklyn Heights nearly every June since I was little Dora, either for camp in Vermont or to travel with the 'rents. Last year, I went on a teen tour of the American West and saw many rock formations.

But this year, I was staying put. Eli, Liza and I hadn't yet spent a summer together. It would be our season, finally. Brooklyn Heights was practically deserted in July and August. We'd own the nabe, roam the city, get great tables at otherwise impossible restaurants, go to free concerts at the band shell in Prospect Park, land jobs at the Smith Street boutiques where we'd get huge discounts and blow our salaries on clothes and shoes. Heaven.

That glittery vision wasn't the kind of summer Mom wanted for me, not by a long shot. Gloria Benet (aka Mater), was twisting the thumbscrews, telling me to get gainful employment, a "character-building job that would look good on college applications." Gloria's fantasy job for me was to volunteer with the Green Project, a coalition of urban farmers whose aim was the building of subsistence organic vegetable gardens on the rooftops of brownstone Brooklyn. It'd be gritty work. Hauling dirt up countless flights of stairs, sowing seeds, rotating crops under the hot sun, tending mulch on burning tar rooftops. In other words, my version of hell. *Anyone's* version of hell.

"I have an announcement to make," said Eli, thankfully bringing my mind back to the air-conditioned comfort at Grind.

"You're pregnant," I joked.

"I'm leaving for the summer," said Eli. "In a few days."

"What?"

"I applied for a spot in the Salzburg Youth Orchestra months ago," said Eli. "It's an eight-week program. High school musicians from around the world come to play in Mozart's hometown. I never thought I had a remote chance of getting an invitation. And then, last week, I got the call." Seeing my expression, Eli added, "I know we talked about spending the summer together in Brooklyn. But I have to do this. I want to do it. I'm really excited."

You couldn't tell from her tone. A stranger who

didn't know Eli would think she was just report-
ing the weather. But I could see through her blank
expression and pick up the faint spark in Eli's dark
eyes, the slight upturn of her lips. Eli was a prodigy, a
New York City high school piano competition champ
many years running. Playing in an international orchestra was a dream come true for her.

Liza gushed, "That's amazing! I'm so happy for
you!"

I said, "Of course, I'm happy for you, too." And
I was.

"Sad for yourself, though," said Eli.

"Your joy is my misery," I said. "Isn't that kind of
sweet, in a twisted way?"

"Whenever I'm homesick," said Eli, "I'll think of
how miserable you are, and I'll feel warm and gooey
inside."

Except for the facts that Eli never felt warm and
gooey—maybe with Charlie—and that she'd never
been homesick, I appreciated the sentiment. I'd miss
her, bad. But I still had Liza.

Liza took a big bite out of her croissant. Her
mouth was partially full when she said, "Mumble,
mumble."

I had to laugh. "You know, that sort of sounded
like you said you were leaving town in a few days,
too. Heh."

"I'm sorry, Dora," said Liza, and then she and Eli glanced at each other.

"Wait a minute. You guys knew about each other leaving?" I asked.

"We live together!" said Liza, as if I needed reminding. When Liza's recently remarried parents moved to Bermuda six months ago, they'd let Liza stay in Brooklyn, living at Eli's house, to finish the school year.

"Where are *you* going?" I asked Liza.

"To Bermuda," said Liza.

"I know *that*," I said. The plan had always been for Liza to go to her parents' beach house for the month of August. She was supposed to stay in Brooklyn for the rest of June and all of July.

"Change of plans," said Liza. "Now that Mom's taken over the administrative work for Dad's snorkeling tours business, they're booking more trips and they need me to help. And, frankly, I want to go. I haven't seen my parents in months. And you know how gorgeous it is right there on the beach. I can't wait to get down there!"

I nodded grimly. It was a gorgeous spot, where Ryan and Stephanie Greene lived in South Hampton. I'd been down there myself this past winter, and hadn't wanted to leave. Honestly, who wouldn't want to go to Bermuda to snorkel all day long?

Come to think of it—"Can I go to Bermuda with you?" I asked.

"I'd love that!" sang Liza. "It's a pretty small house, though. And we'll be working pretty hard. My brother will be there for a few weeks, too. . . ."

"Say no more," I grunted. I could deal with how small the Greenes' house was. But I couldn't be in close quarters with Matt Greene, Liza's brother. I'd had a botched fling with him. It ended badly, and I wasn't in a hurry to see him again.

"Well, this sucks for me," I said. In less time than it took to drink a cup of joe, my vision of the best summer ever had turned into a vast, yawning expanse of lonely months in a ghost town.

Eli and Liza looked at each other again, this time with concern. "We really are sorry, Dora," said Liza. "It just worked out this way."

"We would have told you sooner," Eli said. "But the change of plans happened pretty fast."

"I'm thrilled for you both," I said. "Really, you've got the Summer of Dreams lined up, and I'm jealous as hell. I'll miss you to the point of nausea. Seriously, I'll vomit every morning, thinking of you. But don't worry about me," I said. "I've still got Noel."

Although, to be completely honest, Noel, my boyfriend of nine months, had been a bit of a downer lately. His parents were splitting up, and the town house he'd lived in since birth was on the market.

Potential buyers walked through nearly every day. I'd been a model girlfriend, listening to him (and, let me just say, Noel was a talker's talker), comforting him. I was happy to do it, just as he'd gladly stood by me during a few crises this year at school. But Noel's steady diet of doom and gloom had been wearing. I'd been counting on Eli and Liza to be my fun buddies this summer.

I'd have to recalibrate my expectations. "This could be good, actually," I said. "With you guys off having the time of your lives, I can devote the full force of my energy on Noel. I'll take our relationship to the next level. New heights of emotional connectedness. If you can't have a great summer with your boyfriend, that's pathetic."

CHIRP. My cell. Checking the caller ID, I said, "Speaking of the handsome devil."

"Where are you?" asked Noel in my ear. He sounded testy.

"One guess," I said.

"Good," he replied. "I'm walking in."

And there he was, his lanky frame coming through the door. The sight of him still filled my heart with yummy goodness. He was a sight to behold, a tall, slim, mink-haired, blue-eyed wonder. The most incredible part? He was in love with me. Never ceased to amaze and befuddle practically everyone who knew us, how such a person, a Ruling Classer, could be attracted, body and soul, to a lowly Fringe Dweller such as my-self. He was my superior—in the social hierarchy at Brownstone, in class ranking, definitely in the looks department. I could think of zero areas where I was his better. And yet he loved me. I'd struggled mightily with jealousy during the course of the relationship. If a Ruling Class girl walked within five feet of him, my blood would run green. I realized with relief that all of my competition—Ruling Class Barbies like my sworn enemy, Sondra Fortune—would be gone, gone, gone, all summer long. I'd have Noel to myself.

Yeah, the idea of the major bonding op was grow-ing on me rapidly. I'd redouble my efforts to snap him out of his low-grade depression. We'd have ad-ventures and fun—ridiculous amounts of sex. We'd be a dynamic duo. Even though Eli and Liza would be far, far away, Noel and I could wind up having the greatest adventure of the summer right here in Brooklyn.

I watched, grinning, as Noel made a beeline for our table. He nodded curtly at Liza and Eli. Then he said, "Can we talk?"

"Pull up a chair," I said.

"Alone," he insisted, a weary look on his other-wise dreamy face.

More problems with his parents, I assumed. I lifted my five-hundred-pound backpack and said adios to Liza and Eli.

Noel said, "I'll take that," and lifted the bundle off my shoulders in one clean, effortless jerk. He shouldered the backpack as if it were a sack of feathers, and my heart clenched.

I adored him. I couldn't live without him. And I would show him all summer long.

2

Noel was quiet on the six-block walk to his town house on Pacific Street. He'd taken the sharp turn toward the tacit (a taci*turn*?; note use of SAT prep vocab word) when he had the "Your father and I are getting a divorce" chat with his mom, followed the next day with the "I'm in love with another woman" confession from his dad, and finally, the "We're selling the house" convo with both of his parents. Before his home life collapsed, Noel had been a classroom hand raiser, a blustery, hyperarticulate teacher's pet with an opinion a minute. Since kindergarten, I'd hated his compulsion to share. My feelings changed early this school year, when I realized I didn't actually *resent* Noel for being smart, funny and hot. The long-buried truth? I was in love with him for it! Took me ten years to see the light. Some revelations needed time to wriggle out of the subconscious. Also, I saw Noel naked, which further convinced me of his fine qualities.

"Mom's not home," he said, fitting his key into the lock. "So you can relax."

I exhaled. Belinda Kepner (aka Noel's mater) and I were doing just fine lately, but for a shaky month or so in the spring, we'd squared off. I'd humiliated her in public (by accident!); she'd banished me from Noel's house. Belinda and I made our peace only minutes before she broke the bad news to Noel about the divorce. He never got to enjoy our truce. It was the emotional equivalent of recovering from a cold, only to come down with the flu. I felt horrible for him.

Noel pushed his front door open. I recoiled from the sight. Pre-separation, Belinda had been a pathological straightener, a bored, depressed, pharmed-up housewife who took solace in vacuuming and dusting. These days, Noel's place barely met the neatness standards of a fraternity basement. Piles of newspapers, plates, glasses, mail were strewn on every flat surface. Clothes were scattered about the sofas and tables. Moving boxes were stacked around the rooms, half packed. Dust bunnies multiplied rapidly in the corners.

I glanced at Noel. He looked pained. The mess was the direct result of Belinda's new hobby. She'd become a Match.com dating junkie. Belinda had been out with dozens of men, from all over New York, New Jersey and parts of Connecticut. I'd never seen her smile so much. One time, I picked up the phone and overheard her giggle, then kittenishly breathe the words, "Oh, Jason! That's so *naughty*," before I hung up. It was a wince-worthy moment. On the one hand. On the other, she was hardly ever home since her dating binge began. This bonus far outweighed the mess—for me. And for Noel? Not so much.

I put my finger in his belt loop and asked, "Did she leave money for dinner?"

"I'll just use the card," he said grumpily.

"So what're you in the mood for?" I asked, moving closer.

He kissed me on the lips. It wasn't the kind of kiss that started something. Not something good anyway.

Noel dropped our backpacks in the foyer and then flopped on the plush, shabby chic living room couch. A bit of dust flew up. He said, "I spoke to my dad last night."

"And?" They spoke more since Mr. Richard Kepner moved out than they had in all the years he'd lived here.

"He admitted he feels like shit about what's happened," said Noel. "He blames himself."

I almost said, "He should!" but I bit my tongue. Hard. It bled.

Noel tapped his sneaker toe on the coffee table. "Anyway, he knows he's been an asshole—his word, by the way. He wants to make it up to me. He's taking an emergency family leave from work to do this. Cleared it with Mom."

"Cleared what?" I asked. Noel stared at the tip of his Converse. He wouldn't look at me. That was when my heart sank into my stomach.

"He wants to hike the Appalachian Trail," said Noel. "Not the whole thing. Just the New England portion. From Maine to Connecticut. One thousand miles. We'll carry what we need on our backs, sleep in tents, bathe in mountain streams, wear the same clothes for days."

"The essence of father-son bonding. I can smell it already," I said. "How long will this take?"

"Twelve weeks," he said softly. "We fly to Maine this weekend."

The abandonment was now complete. Every person I held dear was leaving me, and (curses!) each had a good reason to go. How could I rightfully complain, especially to Noel? Twelve weeks, just the two of them, hiking in the mountains? They'd have the chance to say whatever they needed to each other approximately ten million times. Out there, on the long trail, Noel would probably talk to his dad about me. The prospect was both flattering and scary.

"Say something," Noel implored.

"You don't need my permission," I said, kind of bitchily.

"Yes, I do," he said, reaching out, grabbing my wrist and pulling me onto his lap. "I'm not leaving town unless you say it's okay."

This time, the kiss was soft, sweet, a first of many to follow. I said, "It's not okay."

"Dora."

"Seriously, I don't want you to go," I said. "Will you have your cell phone?"

"I'll charge it whenever we hit a town for supplies," he said.

"What if you slide on some rocks, fall off a cliff and die?" I asked.

"Then you probably won't hear from me," he said.

Twelve weeks was an eternity. We'd only been together for nine months, and now he was disappearing for three? Long-distance separations were not generally considered good for relationships. Oh, sure, he'd leave in love with me. I could already picture the tearful good-bye. But would he love me when he returned? And I'd have to wonder about it until he did?

"I should have myself cryogenically frozen for the next twelve weeks. I'll wake up, and it'll be like you never left," I said, pressing against him.

"No, I want you to miss me," he said. "I need to know you were thinking of me constantly. Sitting in a room, daydreaming and writing hundreds of poems about your unfulfilled sexual longing, like Emily Dickinson." He grinned wickedly. "Just think how hot it'll be, the first time after I get back."

And then the real kissing began in earnest. My lips were full steam ahead, but my mind lagged a bit behind. He must've sensed my distraction. He started doing a certain act that he knew riveted my entire mental, physical and emotional attention. I closed my eyes and my brain switched off.

3

"Dora! Thank God you're home. I need your butt," said Joya.

I'd only just walked into my family's duplex apartment on Garden Place, the loveliest of all Brooklyn Heights blocks, to find my younger sister, a rising ninth-grader at Brownstone, sitting on the top of her overpacked camp trunk. The lid was about five inches from closing.

Joya started bouncing on it. She smiled at me like a baby with a new rattle and said, "Weee!" I had to remind myself that she was (1) fourteen years old and (2) my closest genetic link. For starters, we didn't look alike. Joya was a mini-Mom, petite and dark with a heart-shaped pixie face; I was mini-Dad, hazel eyes, honey-colored skin and hair, average height and weight. Also, we didn't think alike. She lived in her fairy land of zombies, mermaids and alien Barbies; I was very much a citizen of the Earth. We definitely didn't smell alike. Thanks to her best friend/boyfriend/only friend Ben Teare, my sister was slathering herself with vanilla extract every morning. Ben thought it made her smell "super sweet," a disgustingly sappy comment that made me gag. Cookies were ruined for me.

"My butt, or anyone's butt?" I asked. "You're not saying I have a big ass, are you?"

"No!" she insisted. "Your ass is super cute."

When had she and Ben started putting "super" in front of every bleeding word? "Just move over," I said, using my *super* cute behind to shove her to one side of the trunk.

My side of the lid did sink lower than Joya's. I could close the latch, but she couldn't. "Both in the middle," I said.

That worked. The lid dropped even farther, nearly close enough to lock.

I said, "On three."

Joya's eyes sparkled. She was in heaven, in the moment. I was a few paces into the future, afraid that on our third bounce, the trunk lid would splinter under us. Mom would blame me for it. Dad would lamely defend me. I'd be forced to apologize to Joya even though it was her idea. She'd accept my apology with a trembling lip and batting giraffe eyelashes. She'd hug me in front of Mom and Dad while they said, "Awww."

"Wait a second," I said.

She wouldn't. "One . . . two . . ."

On three, we bounced. The lid closed. I was ready to snap the central lock in place. Joya quickly fastened the two clamps on the sides. Done. In a few days, she'd be off to art camp in Thetford, Vermont, where she would draw woodland vampire nymphs and eat crunchy, organic food. Most importantly, she'd be three hundred miles away from here. I'd have two blissful months of not being annoyed by her. Mom and Dad would be around, of course. My privacy would be limited. But I kind of liked the idea of it being just the three of us at home this summer. I'd had visions of shopping with Mom, the two of us in and out of stores, carrying bags and boxes, stopping on the way home for coffee, not once discussing my future. We hadn't had a day like that in . . . I wasn't sure. Months. Maybe a year.

With my friends and boyfriend leaving, Mom and Dad would be all I had. I realized with a start that I was the biggest loser in Brooklyn.

"Where are they?" I asked Joya.

"In their office," she said, cocking her head toward Mom and Dad's pocket room at the other end of the apartment. Usually, if they were in there, they were writing one of their best-selling books (*His-and-Her Seduction* and *His-and-Her Dating* had both made the *Times* list) or their *New York Moon* advice column, and not to be disturbed.

"Ben's coming over," said Joya. "It'll be our last night together before the end of summer."

"So he's having dinner with your parents? How romantic," I said.

"Is Noel going away?" she asked. I nodded. "Are you worried about it?"

She caught me at a weak moment. I was dying to talk about it, but I tried to keep the wall of privacy up with Joya. Then again, she was a safe bet for complete sympathy.

"If you weren't the only person around to talk to, I wouldn't be saying this."

"Saying what?" she asked

"What if he forgets me?"

Before Joya could give me a reply that would probably irritate the hell out of me, Mom and Dad's office door opened. Mom came out in the gym shorts and ratty T-shirt she'd slept in, holding the coffee mug that might as well have been fused with the flesh of her hand. Not that Mom was a slob. She was neat as a needle whenever she left the house. On writing days, though, Mom and Dad both got so absorbed in their work that they forgot to shower and dress. Case in point, Dad came out of the office in drawstring PJ pants and a stretched-out Mets T-shirt.

A tag team, they came at me and gave me a suffocating hug. "Congrats," said Dad. "You have passed the eleventh grade. We received the official notification."

"My grades came already? Was I honor roll?" I asked, ever hopeful.

Mom said, "Not even close." Then she grinned at Joya at my left. "Joya was."

Whoa. That was big. "You were honor roll?" I asked.

My sister nodded her bobble head. Diagnosed with ADHD last year, Joya had started taking Ritalin. Her grades surged instantly. All along, we'd thought of her as a lame student. She'd always thought of herself that way, too.

"Nice," I said, genuinely impressed by and, dare I say, proud of her. Joya practically peed herself with gratitude.

"Dora, I want to show you something," said Mom.

She started walking back through the living room, toward the office. I reluctantly followed. Any kind of "business" happened in the office. A one-on-one with Mom in there meant I was going to be on the receiving end of another of her monologues about "the rest of your life."

As soon as she slid the office door closed, she said, "Sit, please."

I took Dad's chair, and mentally braced myself.

"Relax. You look like I'm about to slap you," said Mom. She reached behind her, picked up a stack of papers, and passed it to me.

I read the top line: ADORA BENET. "A resume?" I asked. "When did you do this?"

"Today," she said. "When I got the letter that said you didn't make honor roll—again. Don't mean to rub that in," she added, rubbing it in. "I—we—decided that decisive action is called for. We wrote and printed out three dozen copies of your resume. Tomorrow, you're going to hand deliver them to potential employers."

"What about the Green Project?" I asked, startled by her new tack.

"I—we—changed our minds about that. A volunteer job isn't going to work for you anymore." Mom paused for a beat. "You're hereby cut off. No allowance, no walk-around money. No going to the supermarket for milk with a twenty and keeping the change. Unless you want to eat at home every day and night for the entire summer, you're going to have to get yourself a paying job. No money will flow from me or Dad to you. Consider the well dry."

She had me at "cut off."

"It's not like I'll have any friends to go out with anyway," I said. "They're all leaving town. Eli, Liza, Noel. Gone."

Mom seemed sympathetic, but only for a second. She wasn't going to get dragged to my pity party. She'd obviously prepared this speech (bet if I looked,

I'd find the draft on her computer), and she'd deliver it, by gum, in full.

"You probably think this is harsh," continued Mom, "But it's time you learned . . ."

"You can stop there," I said.

". . . the value of a dollar," she spoke over me.

"I already learned the value of a dollar when you forced me to be your assistant," I said.

"Obviously, the lesson didn't sink in," said Mom. "We also thought that . . ."

"Working some random job would give me fodder for a heartfelt college application essay?" I suggested.

Mom scowled. "It's time you took responsibility for your life, Dora."

The irony of it: I'd already decided to get myself a paying job. I wanted to work, make some money that no one could tell me how to spend. I completely agreed that some real work experience (unlike my cushy job writing a teen advice column for the *Moon*—on hiatus for the summer), would broaden my personal, social and philosophical horizons. I fully intended to announce at dinner tonight—why I'd left Noel's to come home—that I planned to pound the pavement tomorrow in search of gainful employment.

But Mom beat me to the punch. Three minutes ago, getting a job had been my call. But Mom had turned it into hers. Suddenly, I hated my own idea. The rebellious impulse was strong in me, and probably one of the reasons Mom and Dad had reached the end of their rope.

"I'm sorry I've been such a disappointment to you that you feel compelled to disown me," I said, attempting to inflict guilt. Didn't seem to work. Mom's stone face did not crack.

I took my stack of resumes, stormed out of the office and up to my room, where I slammed the door and flung myself on my bed to sob. The tears didn't exactly flow, so I just moaned theatrically for a few minutes, and then contented myself to lie in corpse position, flat on my back, arms and legs immobile, while breathing into my abdomen.

Which got incredibly boring after ten breaths. I scanned the resume Mom wrote. It had my academic history, made mention of my column and my summer travels. I saw she listed my interests as "global warming, endangered species, national debt and gender equality." Channeling herself a bit there. Although who wouldn't say they were "interested" in those things? I was also "interested" in my boyfriend, my friends, Ben Stiller movies, track pants that obscured panty lines, how Splenda was made from real sugar but still managed to have zero calories. But I guess those things wouldn't play on a resume.

Hunger forced me to go downstairs, where my

parents, Joya and Ben Teare were eating a meal prepared by Dad—a tomato paella with shrimp and sausage, the smell of which had been taunting me for an
hour. I loaded a plate and sat down at the table with
as much open hostility as I could muster.

Ben said, "So, Dora. Joya tells me you're worried
Noel will forget you this summer while he's out of
town. I'd be happy to give you a man's perspective
on that."

A *man's* perspective? For years, Eli, Liza and I
called Ben "soon-to-be-gay Ben." If I hadn't caught
them making out on the couch (temporarily blinding
me), I still wouldn't believe he was straight. Ben was
as much of a man as I was.

I glared at Joya. "Hate."

"I had to tell Ben. We tell each other everything,"
she said. "But no one else! I swear!"

"Not even us," said Dad, winking at me.

Mom said, "If you had an absorbing job, you
wouldn't obsess about Noel."

I stood up. "I'll be in my room."

Dad called after me, "Leave your plate in the
hallway when you're done!"

4

The pavement? Not so fun to pound.

The next day, a Thursday (our school ended on a Wednesday; don't ask me why), I put on a denim skirt and clean pink shirt and trudged the length of Montague Street, passing out my resume like a flyer for free pizza. I filled out job applications at a new hamburger-and-fries joint; at a large chain clothing store that catered to hip moms (ugh); at the Hallmark card store that sold Webkins, Beanie Babies and little porcelain statues of angels (I'd shoot myself if I wound up there). Next, I hauled ass up Court Street, filling out applications at a Vitamin Shoppe and the Rite Aid. I ventured along Atlantic Avenue, and begged to apply for jobs at the high-end boutiques and fancy restaurants. But no one would have me. I was too young to serve alcohol, and was therefore blackballed at bistros and tapas bars. At the chic boutiques, my outfit was found wanting. I was given the once-over only halfway before being sniffed at condescendingly and told, at one boutique, to "try Target."

Despite my setbacks, I managed to unload all 36 resumes and fill out a dozen applications by the end of the afternoon. My fantasy—of working at a trendy shop or yummy restaurant—was hereby punctured. The best I could hope for, I feared, was Kinko's. I didn't see how a job Xeroxing other kids' college application essays would provide material for a gripping essay of my own. I pictured myself standing in front of a copier, the light turning my face green, my eyes bloodshot. The tips of my fingers were blackened with printer ink. It wasn't pretty. Reality was "Ugg-*lee*," as I said to myself (unfortunately, out loud, making a few very real people on the street sneer at me).

I was torn from my bleak thoughts by the panting mug of a puppy. He (she?) was jumping around in a box in a storefront window. I looked at his (her?) adorable face, the eyes glistening, nose moist, tongue pink and precious. I melted a bit there on the sidewalk. Having been deprived of a pet my whole life—Mom and Dad were opposed—I was a sucker for the little whelps, especially the helpless, needy kind that could be found in pet stores and shelters.

I glanced at the storefront window, read the name of the place in gold letters. THE FRIENDS ANIMAL

SHELTER. Was it new? I'd never noticed the place
before, and I'd been up and down this block about
a thousand times in my seventeen years in Brooklyn
Heights. I leaned closer to the window and peered
inside. Cages were set up, the names of the cats and
dogs on index cards taped to the metal bars. A for-
tyish, frumpy blond woman in a white lab coat was
pouring dry food into the dishes, one cage at a time.
She'd pause to stroke each animal for a minute. I
could see her lips moving. She was talking to them,
calming them as best she could. It had to be stressful
for the animals to live in cages. A wave of sympathy
for them washed over me.

A man wandered into the cage area. He wore
a white smock, like a doctor, a stethescope around
his neck. I guessed he was the shelter's veterinarian.
What kind of degree did vets have anyway? A V.D.?
Heh.

When the man moved closer to the window and
I got a better look at him, my attention was diverted
from the puppy in the window. I started panting a
bit, watching this guy. He looked like Brad Pitt, only
handsome. I steamed up the window glass gawking
at him. The frumpy blond woman who'd been tending the animals? She was just as smitten, I could tell.
Coy and nibbling her lower lip, she fumbled with the
food bowls when he was near her.

The vet reached into one of the cages and gathered

up a black kitten. He said something to the blonde
and then vanished into the rear of the office, cra-
dling the cat gently, lovingly. I wondered how this
guy might hold a woman. If he'd be as gentle yet
firm.

Before I realized what I was doing, I'd walked
through the shelter door and was asking the smitten,
lip-nibbling, frumpy blonde for a job application.

"I love animals!" I heard myself say. "It's been
my lifelong dream to work with them. I could take
the dogs on walks, and help clean up. Give me a
slotted shovel, and I can scoop cat litter like a
professional."

The woman nodded hesitantly while I babbled. I
pegged her as good with animals, bad with people.
Up close, she was better-looking than I'd initially
thought. But her expression, impatient and haggard,
killed the charm of her pretty eyes and nice skin.

"Do you have any experience handling dogs and
cats?" she asked.

"Not yet," I said. "It's a very sad story, actually. I'd
always wanted a pet, but my parents refused. They
thought animals were a hassle. Which seems very
short-sighted, considering the depth of the relationship between a girl and pet. It's an experience I've
never had, but have always wanted so, so badly." I
gazed with damp affection at the puppy in the box,
and then back at the woman.

She squinted at me, unsure how to take my mercy plea for a job. If only I had a resume left! I could show her that "endangered species" were among my many interests. "Can I run home and get a resume for you?" I asked. "Or, maybe I should just tell you the highlights."

"If you had experience, I'd take your name," said the blonde. "But only for emergencies. We're not hiring. In fact, we've got a waiting list for volunteers. We made our summer hires months ago. I take it you're the last-minute type?"

I frowned aggressively. Was this woman in cahoots with my mother? Was the universe conspiring to make me feel like a slacker? I said, "Thanks for your time," and turned around to leave.

"I'm sure it'll come to nothing," she said, stopping me, "but you can fill out an application if you want."

"You're too kind," I said, taking the white sheet on a clipboard and filling out my contact info. I gave her the paper, paused to give the puppy in the window a nice mini rubdown, and then I left.

I figured I'd never hear from Friends again.

It was a relief that Noel was the first to leave. I hated long good-byes. I hated short good-byes, too. Goodbyes, any length, generally sucked. After my afternoon of looking for a job, Noel and I had our last night together. Unfortunately, this was the rare

evening his mother decided to stay home to spend
a few final hours with her son. We would have to
share him, like a restaurant dessert, forking away
little pieces of Noel until he was gone.

"That's a ridiculous metaphor," Noel said in his
room. I was watching him pack. "For one thing,
you'd never share a dessert."

"I realize this trip is important for you," I said.
"You and your dad need to get to know each other.
He might turn out to be a lover of science fiction. Or
an expert cribbage player. You should pack a deck of
cards, by the way."

Noel said, "Did I tell you he's taking an emergency family leave to do this?"

He had. A few times. Nodding, I said, "You should
take a picture of me to sleep with every night."

Noel said, "I have two dozen on my cell phone."

"How about a special new picture?" I asked. "To
remember me by?"

Noel turned to look at me carefully. Raising an
eyebrow, he asked, "How special?"

I struck poses to amuse Noel. Lots of sexy pout-
ing and back arching. I hoped the pix would not end
up on the Internet.

"Kids?" called Belinda from downstairs. "Food's
here. Come on down."

Another dinner at the Kepners', just the three
of us. Pre-separation, Belinda would have whipped

together a gourmet meal for Noel's last night. Post-separation, the best she would do was order pizza.

"You may never, not ever, even under threat of death, let your father within fifty feet of your phone," I said gravely.

"I'll eat it first," he said.

I laughed, and then burst into tears.

"Come on, Dora," he said, hugging me. "It's only twelve weeks."

I said a hiccuppy "I'm oooooookay." Noel looked at me with love and sympathy. He gave me a tight squeeze.

"We should go downstairs," he said.

I got a grip and nodded. I'd go down, eat pizza, make small talk with Belinda, let Noel go. I'd do it, but I wouldn't enjoy it.

Plus, it bugged me that Noel didn't cry at all, not in his room, and not when, an hour later, he kissed me good-bye at his front door.

Then again, if he had cried, I probably wouldn't have liked that, either. There was no pleasing me.

Friday morning, Mom and Joya drove to Vermont in the packed-to-the-roof Volvo. Dad was designated to stay home. I insisted that I didn't need a parent to babysit me for one bloody weekend. I wound up spending a lot of that weekend in my room, watching my phone not ring off the hook with job offers.

Dad tried to lure me out of my self-pity with what he called "festive summer salads" that usually include raisins. I was regular as a clock by Sunday night, but still staring into the summer abyss—friendless, jobless, but not lacking in dried fruit.

Eli and Liza were both leaving on Tuesday, so we made plans to go out to dinner on Monday. The three of us met at Grind first to pick up Charlie, who was working his final shift as a barista.

"My last day," said Charlie, taking off his visor and apron. "Where did the four months go?"

Eli said, "Any regrets?"

"About this job?" he asked. "No way. I learned how to make espresso, and I met you."

They kissed, deep and true. Liza and I made gagging sounds. They were disgustingly sweet. Eli had fallen hard for Charlie at first sight, mesmerized by his soulful brown eyes; lanky body; long, sexy sideburns and the henna tattoos that circled his bicep. He was older, nineteen, a sophomore at Brooklyn College, and he treated her like the queen of Kings County.

Charlie quit Grind to take a better job as a waiter at the Brick, the restaurant inside the Brooklyn Racquet Club (BRC for short), a fancy, members-only, red brick, federal-style building on Montague Street. The urban equivalent of a suburban golf club, the Brick spanned an entire square block, housing three full-size indoor tennis courts, plus a dozen squash and racquetball courts. A lot of Brownstone Institute families were members. To become one, you had to be invited by other members, supply references and be interviewed by a committee. The fee for membership was in the tens of thousands a year. I wasn't sure of the exact number. Whenever I'd asked my parents, they described it as an obscene amount. That phrase always made me think of a stack of hundreds in a skimpy bra and thong. Charlie got the job through his uncle Jorge Mendez, who managed the restaurant.

"When do you start at the Brick?" I asked.

"Tomorrow morning," said Charlie.

"I've only been inside the building twice," I said, remembering kid birthday parties there years ago.

"It's swank," said Charlie. "But Uncle Jorge keeps the restaurant pretty low-key. Mainly burgers, breakfast, sandwiches. Nothing I can't handle."

"Dora, go talk to him," said Eli, pointing to the manager at Grind. "Ask him for Charlie's job."

Yes! Why hadn't I thought of that? Of course! A job at Grind! It'd be bliss! I already came here every day. But as an employee, I'd get paid. And I'd have unlimited coffee to drink! It was too perfect. My brain simply couldn't process the perfection.

I ran up to the manager, a short, stocky guy with a goatee, named Mr. Aleck.

"I believe, sir, that you are suddenly in need of a

barista," I said. "If the position is available, I'd like to apply for it."

"No, thank you," said Mr. Aleck, dismissing me.

"I'd be ideal!" I insisted. "I know the price and formula for every drink. I could make them in my sleep."

Mr. Aleck said, "Absolutely not. If I gave you this job, you'd drink more than we sell! And you'd sneak drinks to your friends, like Charlie. Business is bad enough during the summer. Losing you as a paying customer? I can't take the hit."

I could see his point. "I'm never coming in here again!" I said. "For as long as I live!"

Mr. (Smart) Aleck bribed, "Not even for a free latte?"

"You can't buy me off that cheap!" I said.

I went back to my crew, told them what happened. "That bastard," I said. "Trying to bribe me with the free latte. Does he think I have no dignity?"

Liza said, "Would he be wrong?"

Charlie laughed. "I'd take the latte now, if I were you. He'll probably forget he offered by tomorrow."

I sighed and said, "Be right back."

After I got my drink, the four of us went across the street to Lantern, a Thai restaurant, where we stuffed ourselves with red curry, pad thai and mango salmon. Liza was a bit antsy to get back to the Stomps' to finish packing. Eli invited me over, but I could tell she and Charlie wanted to spend the rest of her last night alone. I kissed them all good-bye, and walked the three blocks home, dejected and lonely—but optimistic! Something good was bound to happen. Any minute, the phone would ring.

5

Several thousand minutes later, I was still waiting. Mom had been back from Vermont for nearly a week, and she'd made every hour excruciating with helpful suggestions about following up and checking message boards. I'd spent the last few days reading, Googling, watching TV, taking long walks just to get out of the house. I was going a little nuts, actually. I'd decided to print more resumes, psych myself up to re-pound the pavement, when the miracle occurred.

CHIRP. Cell. I flipped it open and said, "Me."

"Dora, come to the Brick."

"Charlie?" I asked.

"Just get over here," he said. "A waitress quit five minutes ago. My uncle is in a panic about being short staffed for the brunch service. I told him I had a friend who needed a job, and he said to call you."

"This is all so sudden," I said. Waitress? At the Brick? I knew a lot of club members from school. It might be embarrassing to serve Brownstoners.

"In ten minutes, he'll come to his senses and wait to hire someone who's got the slightest clue," warned Charlie.

"On my way," I said, bolting out of my apartment and speed walking to Montague Street.

Charlie was waiting at the Brick front entrance for me.

"Nice apron," I said.

He grabbed my wrist and dragged me through the double doors. He guided me past the grandstand tennis court with balcony seating, through the bar area outside the court, presently, at ten on a Saturday morning, crowded with members sipping Bloody Marys and mimosas. I heard the *twack, twack* of a tennis game in progress, and paused to check it out. Charlie said, "Let's GO," and yanked me toward a back stairway, toward the basement kitchen.

"I told Uncle Jorge you had some experience," said Charlie. "Have you ever served food in your life?"

"I worked KP at camp," I said.

"How old were you?"

"Twelve," I said. "But I learned a lot."

Charlie pushed through a set of white doors, and we entered the kitchen. The room was a blinding flash of stainless steel, shiny, bustling with a half-dozen people. The scent of coffee (yea!) and fried potatoes made me instantly glad to be there. The two men in

white caps and white chef coats were standing at a
hot grill. Two women, slightly older than me, in black
slacks, white shirts and aprons, were at a prep table,
filling salt and pepper shakers. The round-bellied,
middle-aged bald guy in a gray summer-weight suit,
with a frantic look on his face, had to be Jorge. The
boss.

He bulldozed over to me and Charlie and said,
"You're Dora?"

"Mr. Mendez," I said, taking his hand, shaking.
"Nice to meet you. I want you to know that I'm
ready, willing and able to do whatever needs doing.
I'm here to work. If you give me a chance, I won't let
you down."

He nodded rapidly, waving me along as I made
my speech. He said, "We open for brunch in half an
hour. I'm one waitress down. I need hands, Dora."

"Got two," I said, holding them up.

"Any food service experience?"

I said, "At camp. I made a hundred and fifty roast
beef sandwiches in less than half an hour. I had a
system, see: I'd lay out rows of bread, and then I'd
squirt the ketchup. . . ."

Uncle Jorge—who must've come from the neu-
rotic side of Charlie's family—looked at his watch,
grimaced and said, "Do you have black pants and a
white shirt?"

"Uh, yeah. At home."

"How long will it take you to change and come back?"

"Fifteen minutes," I said.

"You're hired."

Twenty minutes later, I was behind a butcher-block island, peeling and sectioning oranges to be used as plate garnishes. I wore a pair of too-tight black chinos and a stained white oxford shirt. To my left, a stocky brunette named Rosalyn Mendez was preparing half grapefruits (pitted cherry in the center). To my right, the other waitress, a slim blonde, Stella Walters, was slicing strawberries for plating with French toast. The cooks behind us at the grill—Ramon and Raul Mendez—were frying a wide variety of pork products. I'd gain around twenty pounds in bacon if I managed to keep this job. Despite two large fans, the kitchen was oven hot. I was sweating through my shirt already.

In short order, I got the lowdown on my colleagues. Both cooks were Jorge's nephews, cousins of Charlie's on his father's side. Rosalyn was Jorge's niece, also Charlie's cousin, but not the sister of Ramon and Raul, who were brothers, and cousins with Rosalyn. Follow? Ramon and Raul were older, in their thirties. Rosalyn was a year ahead of Charlie at Brooklyn College.

Except for Stella and me, everyone at the Brick was related, and spoke rapid-fire Spanish.

"Caliente!" I said, when I sneaked over to the grill and pinched a piece of potato.

Raul said, *"Caliente,"* with an authentic accent. He then made me repeat the word until I got it right, by which time the potato had gone *frio*.

Jorge yelled, "Two-minute warning!"

My blood pressure skyrocketed. In two minutes, my professional life would begin. I had no idea what I was doing.

Stella smiled at me, kindly, pityingly. She said, "Do you know the menu?"

"I should read it, right?"

"It's mainly diner standards," she said. "Nothing that needs a crib sheet."

"Okay, thanks," I said, trying to sound appreciative.

She could see, plainly, that I was nervous. To distract me, she asked, "So, Dora, what school do you go to?"

"Brownstone," I said. "It's only a few blocks from here, on . . ."

"I know where it is," said Stella. "I went to St. Andrew's."

St. Andrew's, aka the druggiest private school in New York City, aka "the school for gifted parents," aka Brownstone's bitter Brooklyn Heights rival. Every kid I'd met from St. Andrew's acted like his or her shit was gold plated. Stella didn't seem like an elitist snob. But we'd only just met.

"You grew up around here?" I asked.

"On Pineapple Street," she said. "I graduated from NYU a couple months ago, and I'm back at my parents' for the time being. I'm a singer."

A girl from the hood with ambition in the arts— just like me. I had hopes of living the writer's life. Not following in my parents' footsteps. I'd forge a path of my own, maybe as a novelist.

"I sing a little, too," I said. "In the shower."

She laughed generously, and I took an instant liking to her. I examined her more closely, and noticed how pretty she was. Strawberry blond hair in a high pony, creamy skin, even without makeup. Enviable rack under the staid, starched shirt.

"Where did you go to high school, Rosalyn?" I asked the other waitress, trying to get her in on the conversation.

Her knife moving fast and efficiently, Rosalyn replied, "The Bronx," without looking up from her cutting board.

She made her point—as sharp as the blade. I glanced at Stella, who rolled her eyes at me. I smiled back.

Charlie burst into the kitchen from the dining room through the in door. He'd been setting the tables for brunch service. He grabbed a stack of just-washed butter plates and ran back through the out door, into the dining room.

Jorge was mopping his brow with a napkin. He stared at his watch and shouted, "Thirty seconds!"

Stella wiped her hands and retied her apron. "Do what I do," she said to me. "And if you make a mistake, just smile and beg forgiveness."

"Beg forgiveness?" I asked, taking a pad and pen from a box on the computer stand where we were to log in our orders.

Stella said, "Say a customer orders two eggs over easy, and you bring scrambled. When he complains, say, 'Oh, no! How could I have done such a stupid thing! I am so, so, so sorry. Please forgive me!'" She sounded genuinely upset, and for a second, I thought she was really apologizing to me to for some mystery offense.

I said, "It's okay, don't worry."

Laughing, she said, "See? Act devastated about making a mistake, and they'll start apologizing to you. Play to the customer's sympathy. Gives them a chance to feel superior to you. Sometimes, if you grovel enough, they leave a bigger tip."

Jorge said, "Girls! Stations!"

I followed Stella and Rosalyn out into the dining room. General impression of the space: quaint. Too quaint. Chintz wallpaper, white linen tablecloths. No real windows because it was in the basement, so the room was a bit dark. To compensate, the walls were sunny yellow, with painted green vines and flowers along the wainscoting. The ceiling was sky blue. The room was cozy in decor, expansive in size. I was impressed to count thirty tables. They'd never fill up, I thought.

Stella told me where my section was and which tables I was responsible for. She pointed out the depositories of extra silverware, the roll bin, the butter bucket. Jorge opened the dining room entrance doors. People streamed in and seated themselves.

I gave myself a two-second pep talk. I could do this. I would write down what the customers wanted to eat, and then bring plates to the table. How hard could it be?

Suffice it to say, within a half an hour, I learned just how hard. I won't burden you with the gory details of my performance that morning. Just think of every bad waitress cliché from the movies, and picture me doing them, times ten, including but not limited to:

1. Spilling coffee in a customer's lap

2. Dumping a plate of eggs Benedict on a customer's lap

3. Dropping an armload of dirty dishes on a customer's lap

Notice the recurring theme of soiling the groin

area of people in tennis whites. I must've said a dozen times, "Oh, God! I am such a complete klutz! I am so, so, sosososoo sorry! You should complain to management about me! Get me fired! Right now! I should turn in my apron—or hang myself with it!" The customers didn't act sympathetic to my plight, as Stella said they would. Rather, they tended to recoil with wide-eyed terror.

Anyway, I didn't get fired. For every plate of flying food I made, I managed to properly feed and water the customers at dozens of tables in the five-hour brunch shift. Jorge sweated in my general direction the entire day, shadowing me and fretting. He seemed on the verge of a nervous breakdown whenever I delivered a plate of pancakes. At closing time, however, he visibly relaxed—from basket case to jocular, avuncular nice guy, as soon as the dining room doors closed. He sat down at the nearest table, caught his breath and waited for Ramon to bring him a huge plate of food. It was, apparently, their ritual. All that worrying gave Jorge an appetite, which he sated gluttonously. Stella and I had been taking bites here, bites there, to fuel ourselves for the shift. Seemed much healthier than Jorge's starvation-into-pigfest. But whatever. I enjoyed watching him indulge. He proclaimed each bite a gift from food heaven, showing heartfelt appreciation for Raul and Ramon. Short-order cooks were the unsung heroes of any restaurant, I realized. While Jorge ate, the rest of us cleaned up, refilled ketchup bottles and napkin holders for tomorrow.

Stella pulled out her ponytail holder. Her cut was perfection, a feathery, layered look that framed her oval-shaped face. When she shook out her hair, I heard shampoo commercial music in my head. I caught Charlie watching her, too. And he caught me catching him. He shrugged. I couldn't fault him for staring. Stella was easy on the eyes, compellingly so.

Ramon and Raul were talking to each other while cleaning the grill. Despite five years of Spanish at Brownstone, I picked up one-tenth of what they were saying. Only the obvious words rang clear. *"Esta noche." "Vamos ahora,"* etc. Charlie hardly ever spoke Spanish around Eli and us, so I was *muy impresionada* when he joined his cousins' conversation. Being multilingual was sexy. The word alone was sexy.

I asked Stella, "How long have you worked here?"

"A few months," she said. "My parents are members. They forced me into it. They won't stop me from trying to be a singer, but they won't support me in it, either."

Jorge brought his empty plate in from the dining room. "Seconds?" he asked Ramon.

Rosalyn said, "No time for seconds. I have a ton of homework."

Charlie said, "Give it a rest, Roz. It's summertime."

"Which is why I'm taking only three classes instead of five," she replied.

"Take it easy for once," said Charlie. "You're making the rest of us look bad."

"You weren't looking so good anyway," said Rosalyn with a tongue click.

Ramon and Raul liked her comeback. They howled and gave each other a pound. Ramon said, "Snap!" to Charlie. It was the first English word out of him all day.

Jorge said, "Okay, people. Roz wants to go, we go."

"Uh, excuse me, sir," I butted in. "How does all this work, payment-wise? Do I get a check? Cash? Do we pool our tips and divide them equally?"

"You'll get a check from the Brick once a week for the hourly rate we discussed. If you get tipped on the credit card, that'll show up in your Brick check, minus taxes. Most people know to tip in cash, which you keep," said Jorge. "Just give Ramon and Raul a percentage that you feel is fair."

Stella whispered, *"Twenty percent."*

Nodding, I counted up my cash tips. For my five hours of foot-aching, leg-cramping work, I'd made $139. My by-the-hour wage was a negligible $4.50, an amount that took into account a projected 15 percent in tips. I gave Ramon and Raul a twenty each—roughly thirty percent of my total.

If nothing more, waitressing would be excellent for figuring percentages in my head.

One day, $99 in my pocket. Including my hourly rate, that was roughly $25 an hour.

I was rich! I was rolling in it! I was a wealthy person!

And I'd make around that much—more as I improved—I hoped, every time I worked—four or five times a week. By the end of a week's shifts, I could have $500! By the end of the summer, I'd have THOUSANDS!

"I love this job!" I said, hugging Jorge. "Thank you so, so, sososo much!"

He was so (sososo) surprised by my clench, he dropped his plate.

"I'll clean that up," I said. "Will the price of the plate come out of my check?"

He said, "We'll give you the one plate."

I swept up the pieces. The rest of the crew readied to go. We all walked out together. The Mendezes piled into Jorge's minivan, Bronx bound. That left Stella and me on the Brick stoop, in stained and sweaty clothes, at sixish on a Saturday night.

"You ready?" she asked.

Oh, I was beyond ready—to crawl home, take an

hour-long cool shower, tell Mom and Dad that their daughter was not an unemployable loser after all, that I intended to save up my earnings all summer long, and spend my bundle hiring someone to write my college application essays for me.

I giggled, imagining the horror of their faces. I was kidding, of course. My ultimate goal was the opposite: that one day, in the not-too-distant future, people would pay ME to write. Preferably not college applications.

"I'm ready to take off this shirt and never wear it again," I said. I'd have to get more white shirts. And more black trousers. Mom would agree to pay for those, surely, or my first week's tips were already spent.

Stella smiled at me, disarmingly. My, what pearly, Julia Roberts–big teeth she had. She held up her index finger and said, "One drink."

"I'm seventeen," I said.

"You let that stop you?" she asked. "When I was seventeen, I had five different fake IDs."

The thing about drinking: I'd been drunk about five times in my life at middle school house parties. Getting hammered was surprisingly easy. One drink—a bottle of beer, glass of wine, single shot of booze or snifter of liqueur—would put me under the table. Two drinks would put me under the host (kidding. I should've been so lucky; I saw no action for the duration of middle school). Along with enduring queasiness, drinking gave me terrible insomnia. I'd feel headachy for days. I'd puked at least a little bit in my mouth, if not a lot more, into someone's trash can. I often got chills, and my skin would turn green. In theory, I supported other underage persons sneaking every drop of alcohol they could out of their parents' liquor cabinets. I dampened no one else's blanket. But I did not need alcohol to have a good time. In fact, alcohol practically guaranteed me a very *bad* time.

You rarely heard a lot about famous Jewish drunks. There was a reason for that. As a people, we weren't proficient alcohol metabolizers.

All that said, I didn't want to seem like a dork to Stella—who, meanwhile, was clearly not a Jew. My friends knew me and my half-a-glass alcohol tolerance level well. They found it amusingly incompetent. But Stella was a potential summer pal, someone I felt the instinctual urge to impress. I didn't want to turn her off on our first day. She'd gone to St. Andrew's and NYU. Both big party schools. She naturally assumed that everyone liked a drink after a hard day's work.

One drink (probably) wouldn't kill me. I'd nurse it for an hour, and then go home.

"Where?" I asked.

"I know just the place," she said. "The bartender is a friend. He won't card you."

Stella steered me up Hicks Street, toward Atlantic Avenue. Along the way, she schooled me on waitressing, or what she'd figured out in her two months on the job. I appreciated the advice. But it was a challenge, trying to come off as grateful and attentive when I was exhausted and frazzled. By the time we got to Lester's, a dive bar on Atlantic, I actually needed a drink.

I'd walked by Lester's with Eli and Liza a few times on Saturday nights, the sound of animals being tortured to the tune of "I Will Always Love You" emanating from within. So I knew the place had a karaoke machine. Otherwise, the bar was a mystery to me. I'd always been curious about what the place looked like on the inside. From the outside, it looked pretty lowrent. The window curtains were always closed.

First impression of the interior: dark. The sun was still bright in the early evening, so entering into the dimly lit bar was like stepping into midnight.

"Stella!" shouted a voice. "Get over here! Sit your butt *down*."

My eyes adjusted, and I could make out the man behind the long mahogany bar, arms outstretched. Stella leaned over the bar to give him a kiss on the lips, and then sat down. I took the stool next to her.

Except for a couple at a table by the dartboard, we were the only people there.

"Nick," she said, "this is my friend Adora."

"Dora," I said, holding out my hand.

He shook. "Hello, Dora," he said, his gaze barely leaving Stella's peachy face. This was probably to my benefit. If he looked closely at me, he'd see how seventeen I looked.

"What'll it be?" he asked.

A mirrored wall with glass shelves full of bottles, multihued, beautiful in their rainbow assortment, loomed behind him. There seemed to be a world of opportunity here for drinkers. And for me? A journey into the unknown.

"Vodka tonic," said Stella, dropping her purse on the bar, fishing for her wallet.

"And you?" asked Nick, finally looking at me, raising his eyebrows.

"Uh, I guess I'll have . . . hmmm." I scanned the bottles, wondering what would taste passable. Going for sophistication, I said, "Make mine a white wine spritzer."

Nick and Stella burst out laughing.

"Sorry, Dora," said Stella. "That just sounded so cute."

"White wine spritzer is a punch line?" I said. "Usually, when I'm trying to be funny, I order a rubber chicken."

Nick said, "We're fresh out of rubber chickens. Spritzer coming up."

I spotted the karaoke machine in the back, next to the pool table, and a sign that read KARAOKE SATURDAYS! ONE SONG, ONE DRINK!

"Do you come here to sing?" I asked Stella.

"I come here to make new friends," she said.

I got her meaning, although I didn't think she'd have much luck tonight. The place was dead.

Nick said, "What about your old friends?" To me, he explained, "Stella and I went to St. Andrew's together. A million years ago."

"Did you just graduate college, too?" I asked.

"Last year, from Brown," he said. "Twelve years at St. Andrew's. Four years at Brown. Half a million dollars' worth of higher education. And here I am, serving drinks in a sleazy bar. My parents are so proud."

That made Stella snort with laughter. If I said that, from six blocks away, my mother would hear it, track me to this stool, and slap my face.

"So, tell me, Dora, you must have a boyfriend," prompted Stella.

Okay, getting-to-know-you conversation officially started. I told her about Noel, how we were madly in love, soul mates, destined to be together forever, that nothing could tear us apart.

"I'm convinced," said Nick. "Sounds like you might

have the only high school relationship in history to last longer than three minutes post-graduation."

Stella swatted at Nick. "Don't be an asshole," she said. "Okay, Dora. Observe. My glass, it is full?"

She gestured to her beading tumbler of clear liquid, the lime wedge on top. I nodded, sipping my bulb-shaped glass of wine and seltzer.

"Before this drink is gone, a hot guy will offer to buy me another one," she said.

I scanned the room, at the dozens of empty stools and tables, the absence of even moderately attractive males—except Nick, and he didn't count. "You sure about that?" I asked.

Stella said, "Care to make a wager?"

"First she wants me to drink," I said. "Then she wants me to gamble."

"A gentleman's bet," she said. "Make that a lady's wager."

"You're on," I said.

For the next twenty minutes, I sipped my wine, relieved that it wasn't making me hurl (yet), and listened to Stella and Nick talk about people they knew from high school. Her vodka tonic decreased steadily, with no sign of anyone offering to replenish it. Stella didn't seem anxious or concerned that her bold claim would wind up as empty as her glass.

I didn't understand why, but I started to feel nervous about it. I'd only known Stella for a day. I was halfway to pinning my summer-friend hopes on her. If no guy magically appeared to buy her a drink, she might be too embarrassed to hang out with me again. Or worse, she'd think of me as her bad-luck charm. I slowed my sipping to a glacial pace, trying to draw it out. Not her. Stella drank from her glass with confident gusto.

I said, "You'd better slow down."

She said, "Have a little faith, Dora."

Stella Walters seemed to expect the universe to bend to her will. Well, the universe had better hurry. She was down to one or two gulps left when the bar doors flung open, a swath of sunlight cutting into the dark space. A group of six guys streamed in, one cuter than the next. They wore matching shorts and T-shirts, and each carried a baseball mitt. They were laughing, grass stained, dusty. Obviously, they'd just won their game. I watched them, as a group, push two small tables together and fill the chairs around them. The tallest guy, dirty blond and muscular, biceps bulging under his T-shirt, approached the bar. He stood to my left. To Nick, he said, "Two pitchers of Dogfish Head."

Dogfish Head? Now *that* was funny.

And yet no one laughed. Except me (the spritzer was strong!). The tall guy looked down at me, smiled thinly. And then his eyes skidded across my face and landed on Stella's.

While Nick filled a plastic pitcher with beer from a tap, Bicep leaned against the bar. He waited for Stella to acknowledge him with her eyes.

"How's it going?" he asked.

Stella smiled full wattage at him. She said, "Very badly. Terribly, if you want to know the truth."

The smile contradicted her words. Bicep was confused, intrigued. "And why's that?" he asked.

She held up her almost-empty glass. "Isn't that a sorry sight?"

Nick placed two full pitchers of beer on the bar. Bicep said, "Thanks," and forked over two twenties. While Nick made change, Bicep added, "Another round for the girls, too."

And just like that, Stella's promise came true. Right under the wire. Like magic. She winked at me, not subtly *at all*. Bicep saw it. I thought he'd be insulted. But he seemed amused by the idea that he'd just been manipulated. He delivered the two pitchers to his friends at the tables—who were loudly celebrating their victory on the playing field—and then Bicep returned to the bar to sit on the other side of Stella.

Nick served us our fresh drinks. I noticed that mine was heavy on the seltzer, only a splash of wine for color. I smiled at him in gratitude. He leaned over the bar and whispered, "I charged him full price."

For the next hour, I watched Stella at work. An

amateur waitress, she was a master seductress. Although she tried to get me involved in her conversation with Bicep a few times, I felt like an intruder on their instant intimacy. She spoke softly, so he'd lean in closer to hear her. When he spoke—about the game he just pitched, his apartment in Boerum Hill—Stella stared at him like a dazed deer, big eyes and innocence, with a slightly wild edge.

I knew if I tried that wild-eyed gaze, I'd look like an escapee from a mental hospital. Stella, however, appeared stunned by her sudden, deep attraction to this incredible man who'd miraculously walked into her life.

Forget job tips. I'd rather Stella gave me a primer on flirting with boys in bars. A sickening thought: I wondered if Stella got any of her tricks from Mom and Dad's best-seller, *His-and-Her Seduction*. Another unsettling notion: Did girls like Stella put their moves on Noel when he and Stanley went to bars?

That revolting thought was enough to put me off my seltzer. I made my excuses and got up to go. Stella said, "You're not leaving!"

I said, "I'm just really tired."

She begged, "Hang out, Dora. Please."

At first I thought she really wanted me to stay. But then I understood the truth.

Bicep said, "Don't worry, Stella. I'll keep you company."

Stella said, "But, Dora . . ."

I played my part. "Next time, I'll close the bar with you, I promise."

I headed out. The bar was crowded now, and I had to wind my way through the crush. I looked back once. Bicep had brought Stella over to the table, to the only empty chair around it. He offered it to her; she offered it to him. They smiled at each other. Then, wordlessly, he sat in the chair, and she sat on his lap.

6

June 26, 2008
To: estomp@brownstone.edu
From: abenet@brownstone.edu
Re: How much your boyfriend rocks

Eli: I'm madly in love with your feller. He got me a job! I heart the job. Ergo, Charlie Mendez is my hero. I am now an employee at the Brick, serving hot griddle cakes to rich people in short white pants. I've got four or five shifts per week, and waitress alongside Charlie and two girls. Rosalyn, Charlie's cousin, hasn't revealed her friendly side to me yet. The other, Stella, had generously stepped into the vacant spot as my "friend." She's cool, a singer (sounds good in the kitchen), and a bona fide babe magnet. I went out with her twice after work. She walks into a bar, and it's Attack of the Killer He's. Men SWARM. She's got strawberry blond hair and a nice smile, but I wouldn't call her gorgeous. Maybe she pumps out invisible pheromones only men can smell. Wonder where I can get some. Meanwhile, Noel? Has not called, e-mailed, texted or sent a carrier pigeon. It's been nearly two weeks since he left.

June 27, 2008
To: abenet@brownstone.edu
From: estomp@brownstone.edu
Re: schnitzel

You won't recognize me when you see me. I've gained five pounds already. Five pounds of pastry, schnitzel and big, soft pretzels that make the NYC street nosh pretzels taste like cardboard. Salzburg is old. I used to think Brooklyn Heights was old because I live in a 150-year-old town house. My Salzburg house is 400 years old. About as old as the couple who are my Austrian "parents." If they die while I'm living here, my summer would definitely suffer. Every morning, when they wake me up, waving cream puffs in my face, I'm relieved they got through the night. Charlie e-mailed me about your girl crush on this Stella person, and that you aren't paying nearly enough attention to him at work. Is Stella your NBF? Good, because you were in desperate need of someone to talk about Noel to. Re: Rosalyn. Met her. Liked her. She's very serious about school. Laser focused. It's a bit pathological, but who am I to judge? Don't worry about Noel. He's communing with nature and his father. Eventually, he'll cross paths with two woodchucks going at it, and he'll think misty, dewy, loving thoughts of you.

June 29, 2008
To: lgreene@brownstone.edu
From: abenet@brownstone.edu
Re: floating pool

Liza: While you are cleansing your soul in the Atlantic Ocean, I will have you know that I, too, have been enjoying immersion in purifying waters. And I don't mean my bathtub. The big news around here is the recently parked Olympic-size swimming pool on a giant barge just off the Brooklyn Heights pier, a mere five-minute walk down Joralemon Street from Garden Place. It's totally FREE (my favorite word), open to the public, seven days a week. I've been going in the mornings for the first swim of the day with a girl from work at the Brick. Her name: Stella Walters. She has replaced you and Eli in my heart—if only for the next two months—which is the thanks you get for leaving me, you bitch. I forgive you, btw. In fact, I am wishing you happiness, confidence and a summer fling. I have visions of you running down the beach in a bikini, hot guys spinning around to check your butt as you jog by. I bet you hair is white blond from the sun. Honestly, I miss you in the guts.

June 30, 2008
To: abenet@brownstone.edu
Fr: lgreene@brownstone.edu
Re: your guts

Are they all twisted and tight? If so, I recommend bran muffins and an apple, every single day. I laughed at your vision of me running down the beach. FYI: I don't run. Anywhere, and definitely not on the beach. And, two: me, in a bikini? The guys would stop and stare—in shock and horror. Actually, all the fresh fruit for breakfast has probably made me lose a few pounds, exactly where I need it (that being in the bikini bottoms). It's been awesome to spend such intense family time. Dad is great, the same. Mom is a changed woman. She's totally adapted to the beach-bum lifestyle. Take a woman out of the city, the pantsuit, the cubicle, and there's no going back. It's been over two weeks and I haven't seen Mom cry once. It's like she's had a personality makeover. This will shock and amaze you, so you'd better sit down: I heard Mom singing to herself this morning while scrubbing dishes. Kills me how unhappy she must have been for YEARS after Dad left. Now they're back together, and all is well. Eli said you haven't heard from Noel. Do not worry! I'm sure he's thinking about you all the time, because he loves you and misses you, as I do. Not in the same way, of course. But I do miss you and love you lots.

[POSTCARD STUCK ON FRIDGE WITH A MAGNET. COVER IMAGE: A PAIR OF BARN OWLS SITTING ON A TREE BRANCH, STARING EERILY STRAIGHT AHEAD, PIERCINGLY, AS IF THEY COULD SEE YOUR BONES. ON THE FLIP SIDE, A HAND-SCRAWLED MESSAGE.]

Hi, everyone! Do you dig the owls? I'm going to make a clay sculpture of them, their faces, on the bodies of twin human babies. Cool/weird, right? Art camp is great so far! I like all the girls in my bunk except one, Olivia. I saw her stealing Twizzlers from Amy's care package. Can you send me new jeans? I painted my old ones. They're art now, and I need a pair to wear. Also, send comics, Doritos and the stuff you put on mosquito bites. After Bite? XXXOOO, J.

"Yup, you've come to the right place! It's Noel's voice mail! And you should really leave a message, as soon as you hear the . . . *BEEEEP!*"

"It's Dora. Again. I'm calling you, clogging your mailbox with the enormity of my NEED to hear your

voice. Call me insecure! Call me clingy! Just frigging
CALL ME, Noel. I hope you're having a swell time
with your dad, and that you haven't had to eat tree
bark or drink your own blood to survive. Okay. Bye.
Love you."

7

"You're going to spy on me," I said, hands on my hips, my beach bag over my shoulder.

"That's ridiculous," said Mom, putting an extra towel into her beach bag and tugging at the strap of her (God help me) red bikini top. "We turned in our column. It's ninety degrees, and we thought we'd take a swim. Besides, we're curious about the floating pool."

"How convenient for you," I said. "You'd fool a lesser daughter. But not me. What you're *really* curious about is my new friend Stella. Whether she's a positive influence on me."

"Well, we would like to get a look at her," admitted Dad, in surf-style swim trunks that fell to his knees.

"I knew it! It is all about me!"

"Who says teenagers aren't self-absorbed?" asked Dad.

"Just pretend you don't know us," said Mom.

I felt a headache coming on, possibly from caffeine withdrawal, probably from parent overdose. "Let's make a vow to respect each other's privacy," I tried.

They laughed out loud at that.

"I'm leaving now," I said, disgusted. "You guys have to wait ten minutes before you leave."

"Don't be ridiculous," said Mom, shouldering her bag and pushing me and Dad out the door.

We walked down Joralemon Street, toward the piers of Brooklyn and the floating pool barge. Mom and Dad acted as excited as little children. They held hands and swung their linked arms back and forth. Granted, they'd been cooped up in their stifling office for days, finishing their column. It was only natural they'd be giddy for free time, fresh (if hot and humid) air. But they were my parents. They were acting like lovesick teenagers. And that made my cheeks throb with embarrassment. When we arrived at the entrance to the pier, Dad said to the parking lot attendant, "We're not with her. She doesn't know us, and has never met us before."

The attendant said, "I've never met my kids, either, when we're in public."

Oh yes, parents from all walks of life were united in the pleasure of mortifying their children.

I scanned the "beach" for Stella. It wasn't a real beach, or anything close. The barge people had trucked in thousands of pounds of sand, and poured it in the parking lot to simulate a beach experience. You could rent an umbrella for twenty dollars an hour and hang at the "beach" all day if you so desired. Most people used it as the waiting area. Only seventy-five swimmers were allowed on the pool barge at a time. The officials handed out color-coded wristbands for each hour-and-a-half time slot. If you were swimmer number seventy-six, you had to wait until the next swim period. On lunch-shift days, Stella and I met on the "beach" half an hour before the first swim of the day at ten o'clock, to make sure we got wristbands.

And what did we do while we waited on the sand pile? Stella and I talked. Well, mainly, she talked. I listened. Her life was much more eventful than mine. Stella went out every night. Incredibly, no matter how wasted she got, she always looked great at 9:30 in the morning.

Eli had said I had a girl crush on Stella. Some truth to it. When she told her stories, about the handful of men who vied for her attention the night before, I felt a little bit jealous. Of the guys. Stella was so excited by their fawning. When she turned that excitement toward me in the retelling, I responded in an almost romantic way. Not sexual. I didn't want to kiss her. I think the romantic feeling, for me, was wanting to be like her. Imagining that the girl everyone wanted, wanted to spend time with me. Or maybe Stella just

embodied a feel-good happy vibe. In old movies, she
would've been called a bon vivant. A free spirit. My
spirit, in comparison, was dearly expensive. I saw the
high cost of every action. Staying out late? Drinking until hammered? Spending money on taxis and
night club covers? Flirting with strangers? That all
went against my Brownstone training about personal
conduct. Oh, I could do it all. But I'd have guilt. St.
Andrew's, apparently, had ignored instilling a sense
of guilt as part of a student's education.

I was both envious and appalled by Stella's overt
flirtation, what I'd heard in her stories, and what I
witnessed at Lester's and the Brick. Although several
guys had tried to seduce me this past year, none of
them came at me cold. They got to know me first
and decided they liked me. Boys didn't zero in on
me at first sight. They barely noticed me, actually.
Stella, though, had a figurative target painted on her
forehead. I wasn't immune. Her sex appeal attracted
me, too.

Walking as fast as I could to put distance between
me and my parents, I scanned the "beach" loungers
and spotted Stella immediately. She wore a look-at-
me-don't-look-at-me wide-brimmed hat, big black
sunglasses and a sheer white cover-up that somehow
made her look naked. Trudging across the sand, I felt
the flutter of relief. She hadn't blown me off, as I
feared she would, every time we had plans to meet.

"Hey," I said when I was close enough. I dropped my bag on the sand next to her and rummaged for my towel. I spread it out and lay down on it. Stella was leaning up on one elbow. She smiled weakly at me. The sunglasses hid her eyes, but she still looked tired.

"This might be the worst hangover of my entire life," she moaned.

Today, for a change of pace, I was determined to steer the conversation away from her drunken club crawls and toward my short list of problems. Namely, the sad fact that Noel hadn't called me since he'd left Brooklyn. Objectively, I didn't believe he'd fallen off a cliff, his body consumed by rabid chipmunks and badgers. Or that he was intentionally blowing me off. The problem wasn't that he hadn't called—the guy was probably out of range, for one thing—but that I couldn't control my hurt feelings about it.

Before I got the chance to say anything about Noel, Stella lowered her glasses and asked, "Dora, are those your parents?"

She was looking at the concession stand, where you could buy croissants for five dollars and lame coffee for three dollars a cup, no refills. Mom and Dad were leaning against the stand, stirring Splenda into their styrofoam cups, watching us. When they saw me turn toward them, they looked away and stared into their cups as if the meaning of life could be found inside them.

Smooth, I thought.

"Please ignore them," I said.

Stella sized up the situation quickly. "They've come to check out your new friend?" she asked. "Don't roll your eyes. It's cute, Dora. You look *exactly* like your dad. And your mom is so tiny!"

Implying that I was a galumphing water buffalo in comparison? "My sister Joya looks like Mom," I said.

"Call them over," said Stella, sitting up with a straight spine, getting into meet-the-parents posture. I hesitated, so Stella took it upon herself to wave them in.

Dad smiled and waved back, really big, wheeling his arms. Mom said something to Dad, and he dropped his arms and put his hands in his pockets. Then they headed over.

Silently, I prayed this would end quickly.

"Stella Walters, I'd like you to meet Gloria and Ed Benet," I said.

Mom held out her hand. Stella gamely shook it. And then Mom shifted directly into Inquisitor Mode. She used her trademark sympathetic and respectful tone. It had a lulling effect that made just about anyone open up to her. I secretly hoped Stella wouldn't be an easily cracked nut.

"Stella, we heard you want to be a singer! That's fascinating. I wish I could sing, but I'm totally tone deaf," said Mom. "It must be hard, facing so much rejection."

Stella laughed. "Rejection? What do you mean?"

Mom said, "Auditions, tryouts, that sort of thing. Isn't that how it works these days?"

"I couldn't tell you, Gloria," said Stella, using Mom's first name. "I haven't really gotten into the thick of auditioning yet. I'm still working on my sound, my performance. I do a lot of open-mike nights at clubs for practice."

Dad said, "Do you get paid for open mikes?"

"The opposite," said Stella. "To sing, you have to buy drink tickets. You have to get your *friends* to buy drink tickets. It's a total rip-off. But it's worth it for the onstage experience. I'm singing this weekend, the night of July fourth, at Magna Mango in the East Village." To me, she added, "I want you to be there, Dora. You have to come! I'm dying for you to hear me sing."

"Is this a bar?" asked Mom.

"Of course not!" said Stella. "I'd never take Dora to a bar. That would be against the law. Besides, I hate bars. If it weren't for open-mike nights—at other places, not where I'm performing next week— I wouldn't step foot inside a bar again." She smiled at them beautifully, like an innocent little lamb.

Props to Stella for trying, but no way were my parents going to buy that act. I watched Mom and Dad smile back at her, nodding like they were lapping up the Kool-Aid. But underneath? So not.

Dad said, "We usually spend the fourth on our roof. We have a great view of the fireworks."

Mom said, "Dora is too old to watch the fireworks with us, Ed."

"She did last year," he said.

We'd all climbed the vertical ladder to the hatch door, climbed up onto the roof to ooh and ah as explosions shot from barges on the East River, not very far from where we were right now. The fireworks were loud and bright, right over our heads, as if the fireworks display watched by all of America on TV was actually a private show just for us. Our roof was crowded. Eli, Liza, Joya, me, Mom and Dad, Dr. and Mrs. Stomp, Stephanie Greene. Up and down our row of brownstones, we could see and hear our neighbors applauding and cheering from their roofs.

So much had changed since last July. Noel was barely a blip in my consciousness then.

I said, "People are starting to line up."

The queue to get on the pool barge was forming. Mom and Dad got all jumpy, like they might not get on if they didn't rush over there. They excused themselves and ran to get a place. Stella and I took our time, waiting for the line to start moving.

"They're cute," said Stella. "Do they always hold hands like that?"

I cringed. "They don't realize they're doing it."

"You're lucky to have parents who are so together," said Stella.

"Too together," I said. "The his-and-her lifestyle is a bit hard to take sometimes." I hoped Stella would nip at the bait and tell me about her parents, the rent-chargers who were rarely home. As open as she was about her social life, Stella corked up about her family. The contradiction was glaring. She would give graphic descriptions of her intimate adventures, but everyday domestic details were off-limits.

"We'd better go," I said, watching dozens of people walk up the gangplank to the pool. We got wrist-band numbers 72 and 73. Just made it.

On the barge, we arranged our towels on the patio in our usual spot. After twenty minutes of baking on the "beach," I was beyond ready to dive in. I kicked off my flip-flops, and ran toward the water.

A whistle blew. "You! In the green!" said a life-guard into a bullhorn. "No running!"

I realized seventy-five pairs of eyes were fixed on my green tank suit. "Sorry!" I said lamely, and walked, slowly, to the edge of the pool. I jumped in. When I surfaced, Stella's body was flying over my head. She splashed down a few feet away. Water went up my nose. When she surfaced, she was already laughing.

"Did I get you?" she asked.

Did she get me? And I meant that in the figurative sense. I wasn't such a deep enigma. But, honestly? She didn't know all that much about me.

"You got me, all right," I said, blowing my nose.

Whistle again. "You! In the green!" said the bullhorn-happy lifeguard. "No blowing your nose in the pool!"

Scores of bobbing heads turned toward me, in the green, including my parents, who looked horrified.

"I sneezed!" I said. "It was an accident."

Stella said, "Jeez, Dora, can't you keep your snot to yourself?"

I agreed to try. We splashed around for a while, floated along, dunking occasionally. Men of all ages noticed Stella. I noticed that they noticed. A couple of guys, young and ripped, had been staring at her since we jumped in. If we were at a bar, they'd've already bought her a drink. Here at the pool, I couldn't guess how they'd try to get her attention, but they surely would. I braced for that, when Stella would turn her attention toward the interested males, soak up their admiration like a mop, and forget about me.

"Check out your parents," she said.

I scanned the bobbing heads until I located Mom's and Dad's. Mom had her arm around Dad's shoulders, and he was carrying her through the water. Occasionally, he'd dunk her, she'd sputter and laugh, they'd kiss.

"That's the real thing," said Stella.

Meanwhile, the two ripped guys were making their move. Diving under the water, they surfaced a few feet away from us. "'Sup?" asked the first guy, raking his wet hair back over his head. Up close, I saw he had a whispery mustache (HATE!). He had a few zits on his cheeks, and could be anywhere from sixteen to twenty.

His friend—clean shaven, smaller in build, with sweet brown eyes—asked, "Swim here often?"

Stella groaned theatrically. "Can't you see we're having a conversation here?" she said. "What gives you the right to interrupt us anyway? And why on earth would we want to talk to *you*? No, don't answer that. Just get lost. You're annoying us."

At first, they were shocked. Then they got pissed. "Fuck you, too," said the whisper 'stache. "Dyke."

"Asshole," Stella spat back. Not real spit, of course. We'd have gotten the bullhorn treatment. She used the dreaded spit *tone*. It worked. They cursed at us some more and then swam away, sufficiently emasculated.

Stella hoisted herself out of the water and sat on

the pool's edge. "Sorry about that," she said. "I hope I didn't embarrass you."

"No!" I said. "They were embarrassed. I was impressed."

"I'm just not up for it this morning, you know?" she said. "Guys will hit on you anytime, anywhere. It can get annoying. Depressing. It's constant pressure."

"Guys will hit on *you* anytime, anywhere," I corrected. "They tend to be a bit more discriminating with me."

"And you'd love it if guys were all over you?" she asked. "It sounds fun if you're not used to it. But trust me, the guys who hit on me are never the ones I want."

"Never?" I asked.

"Well, hardly ever," she conceded. "Like last night. I was at Lester's, and this guy, Roy, walked in. Nick introduced us. Roy runs an Internet company from his apartment. When he went to the bathroom, Nick told me he's loaded."

"And instantly, he got a lot better-looking," I said.

"It's amazing how that happens," said Stella, her eyes gleaming. "Roy and I got to talking, and he offered to design a Web page for me. So I went to his apartment on Warren Street, to check out his operation. . . ."

I listened to another story of seduction and conquest

and modest reward. Stella always seemed to walk away in the morning with some small bone to chew on—in this case, a promise to build her a fan site when her career took off. By the time she finished her Roy Toy tale, the whistle blew and the lifeguard blasted, "Time's up, people! Get out of the pool!"

8

"Where is everyone?" I asked Jorge. It was the morning of July 4. I'd assumed the Brick would be busy.

"It's the Friday of a holiday weekend," he said. "Everyone leaves town."

And when he said "everyone," he meant rich Brick members who had summer retreats in Connecticut and Duchess County. About half of Brownstone families had second homes. Not us. Mom and Dad sold a lot of books, but not enough to support two houses, school tuition and trips. Eli and Liza didn't have country houses, either, so I never felt the lack.

I did today, though—the lack of customers to serve, the lack of tips, the lack of decent conversation in the kitchen while we waited for someone to feed. Rosalyn and I were the only waitresses scheduled for the slow start of the holiday weekend. Stella was preparing for her gig tonight. Charlie had the day off. He was going to meet me in Manhattan later at Magna Mango to see the show.

"You should come, too," I said to Rosalyn, as we lazily chopped celery and carrots. "I feel like we haven't gotten to know each other at all. We can hang. You can tell me funny stories about Charlie as a kid, and I'll pass them along to Eli."

"No, thank you," said Rosalyn.

"Come on," I said. "You need to get out more."

She snorted. "You think you know what's good for me, Dora?"

"You're very defensive," I said. "And that means I'm right."

"Why would wasting my time and money at a noisy club in the city be good for me?" she said.

"You'll get to hear Stella sing," I said.

That made her double snort. "No comment."

"I'll pay for you," I said. "It's a five-dollar cover, and two-drink minimum." I reached into my trouser pockets and found a few crumpled fives. "Here's fifteen."

That made her put down the knife. "Why do you want me to go so badly?" asked Rosalyn, her brown eyes boring into mine.

The answer: guilt. Among the female waitstaff, Stella and I had hit it off, but Rosalyn and I hadn't. Granted, she didn't seem to care. But I knew she had to, even a tiny bit. It was only human nature to feel the sting of being left out. The exclusion wasn't malicious. It was largely self-inflicted. I invited Roz along whenever Stella and I went out after work. She always said she had studying to do.

"Just go, Rosalyn," said Jorge. Rosalyn's uncle was a talented, bilingual eavesdropper. All this time, I thought he'd been totally absorbed in the newspaper. "You're a beautiful young woman, and you live like an ugly spinster. Go out, have fun."

"Convengo totalmente," said Ramon from behind the grill.

Roz said, "Shut up, Ramon."

"Fifteen bucks," I said, waving the fives in her face.

Rosalyn snatched the bills and said, "You will pay for this, Dora. With money, too."

"What kind of skank joint is this place?" asked Rosalyn a few hours later when we arrived at Magna Mango on St. Mark's Place.

More like a "stank" joint. The odor of mung beer seemed to emanate from the walls. And, on second thought, the patrons were kind of skanky, too. In five seconds, I counted more cropped tops and tattoos than I'd see in a week in Brooklyn Heights. But this was to be expected. We were in the East Village of New York, epicenter of body-art culture; birthplace of the pierced eyebrow; home of punks, junkies and

hipsters and sidewalk drug dealers; the choice desti-
nation for tourists in search of vinyl underpants. The
East Village was also famous for being the easiest
neighborhood in New York to buy pot on the street,
and to get served.

From the outside, Magna Mango didn't look too
bad. A neon sign with the bar's name hung over a
red painted door. No homeless people or frightening
street people lay about the entryway. Going by the
collegiate crowd gathered out front, the club seemed
as respectable and low-key a bar as you could hope to
find in this part of town.

From the inside, the club's collegiate vibe took
a sharp turn toward the sleazy. Goth girls in layers
of black lace sat atop rusty metal stools at the bar.
Long-haired alterna-dudes in ripped T-shirts, matte
leather jackets and filthy high-tops lined up against
the shiny walls. Seating was limited. The scant tables
and chairs were filled with human-shaped shadows.
Music blared. I recognized the plaintive wail of the
Killers. I liked that, at least. The smell, the press, the
nose rings and greasy hair all around me? Not too.

As a lifelong Brooklyn Heights resident, I realized
I'd been sheltered. My neighborhood was an urban
Disney World—clean, friendly, upscale—compared
to this raw slice of city life. A lot of Brownstoners
loved coming to the East Village to dance and drink
and then take taxis home with the last of their crum-

pled singles. Eli, Liza and I tended to roam in our own borough, opting for coffee and french fries over beer and bong hits. Now I knew what I'd been missing: an assault on the senses, a gritty *mise-en-scène* that made me want to shower. Yet the grunge was oddly appealing, if only in contrast to the order of my usual existence. In Brooklyn Heights, things got messy in the metaphorical sense only.

"Shall we get messy?" I asked Roz, feeling a little dangerous.

"You get messy," she said. "I'll try not to watch."

"Hey, guys! Over here!" It was Charlie, at the bar, squeezed between two emo girls in severe makeup.

Rosalyn frowned. "Are you drinking *beer*?" she asked her cousin.

"So?" he said, instantly embarrassed.

"You're underage!" said Rosalyn, loud enough for the bartender to hear.

"Chill out, Roz," said Charlie, sneaking a look at the girl to his left, the one now snickering at him. "If that's possible."

"Where's Stella?" I asked Charlie.

"What?" he asked.

"Stella?" I shouted so he could hear me.

He pointed toward another section of the club. "By the stage," he said. "Surrounded by her posse."

No doubt, a throng of male admirers. I gestured to the cousins that I was going to look around, and pushed my way through the crowd, deeper into the club.

The back room had a low-rise stage with a mike stand, some sound equipment and a drum kit. More seating options back here, but all the chairs and tables were packed. Even in the dark room, among the crowd of people dressed in various shades of black, I spotted Stella almost instantly. The eye just went to her. Also, to enhance her natural attention-getting properties, she wore a silver sequined minidress that reflected the scant light, turning her into a human disco ball.

Like a ship in a storm, I steered toward her light. As I'd predicted, she was surrounded by guys, and girls, too. She seemed to know them all. When she saw me pushing through the crowd, she pointed to me, and a dozen pairs of eyes turned to look. They seemed unimpressed by my ensemble of jeans and a pink trapeze top. Too princessy, I guessed. Oh, well. Next time, I'd dress like drug addict.

"Guys!" sang Stella. "I want you to meet Dora Benet. She's made my waitressing job bearable."

She made introductions. I couldn't hear the names, but I got the associations. Most of them were friends from NYU, a few from St. Andrew's. All of them older than me, with a crusty patina of ennui.

"Make room," said Stella, nudging her pals. "Have a seat, Dora. The show starts in a few minutes."

A few minutes turned out to be an hour. During that time, I sat among Stella's friends and observed. They talked across me as if I weren't there, the conversation full of references to events and people I didn't know. Self-conscious, I laughed when they laughed, nodded when someone told a long story, smiled woodenly, hoping Stella and her peeps tolerated me at least. I felt like a lump, sucking up the club's thin oxygen, offering nothing in exchange. Overall, I'd describe the experience as extreme self-conscious awkward discomfort. Wedged tight in the booth, I started to get thirsty. So thirsty that, when a guy brought a pitcher of beer to the table and Stella pushed a plastic cup at me, I drank it in one gulp.

Stella refilled my cup. By the time I finished that beer, I wasn't feeling quite as conspicuous. My laughter sounded less canned. My smile was genuine. My bones relaxed, and Stella's pals seemed less scary. The guy next to me—Brian?—another former music major at NYU, whispered in my ear, "Are you cold?"

I said, "It's a thousand degrees in here." He put his arm around me and rubbed my bare shoulder anyway.

The music stopped suddenly. A guy in a Ramones T-shirt and inky skinny jeans jumped onstage. Stella smiled broadly at her friends and said, "Here we go."

"Can I get the band onstage?" asked the Ramones

guy into the live mike. A few people climbed onto the stage and plugged in their instruments. A girl drummer—I liked that. Two dirtbag-ish guitar players, and a Mod bassist.

Stella called out, "Stephan!" She waved frantically. The grungier guitar player with jet-black hair looked over and cocked his chin at her. She acted flustered and pretended to faint, which made the girls in the booth laugh and the guys frown.

The MC announced the club's upcoming schedule of bands and then explained how the open-mike night would proceed. "I'll call out names from the sign-up sheet in random order. When you hear your name, come up and sing one song. The singer who gets the biggest applause gets to come back and do a whole set on a night to be named in the near future."

Stella said, "You guys better scream for me."

Brian (?), the guy who was now aggressively rubbing my back, said, "Only if you scream for me later."

"In your wet dreams," said Stella lightly, no offense meant or taken. How did she *do* that? I wondered. Insult someone, and make it come off like a kiss.

I—everyone—had to endure the warbling performances of a half-dozen singers. The range of songs was vast. One woman sang "Memory" from the Broadway show *Cats*. A guy got up there and bellowed into the mike what was supposed to be "Whole Lotta Love" by Led Zeppelin. The house band played every song the singers threw at them. If they didn't know it already, the musicians sounded out the melody spontaneously. A musical misfit, I was in awe. New York City was a dense forest of talent. Shake a tree, and a genius would fall out.

Forty-five minutes went by, and Brian (?) moved his massage hand from my back to my thigh. He didn't ask me if it was okay (as per the Brownstone training on sexual etiquette). He barely even looked at me. He could have been mindlessly groping a blow-up doll. When his hand inched up my leg, dangerously high, I had to move. Excusing myself, I scrambled out of the booth.

Stella looked at me, her eyes pleading, "You're not leaving."

"I need air," I said. The three beers were making me queasy. I must've glanced nervously at Brian (?), too.

Stella caught it. "You loser," she said, her head swiveling toward Brian (?). "Keep your lechy hands to yourself. She's just a kid!"

Just a kid? Was that so? I thought I was her equal. Her comrade in aprons. The swift downgrade from "workplace savior" to "just a kid" made my head spin. The close air in the windowless room didn't help, either. I felt a bit of sick on my tongue. I backed up a few steps, out of Stella's line of vision, but still close enough to hear one of her other friends ask, "Why did you invite that girl anyway?"

Stella said, "She looks up to me. I need that kind of love flowing my way tonight."

So there it was. I was her confidence delivery system. I fed her hungry ego. I could have been watching the fireworks on my roof in the company of my parents. Which would have made me a geek and a loser, but at least I'd've been able to breathe. Attempting to turn around and go, I stumbled backward and collided with someone.

"There you are," he said. I'd stepped on Charlie's toes.

"Watch the leather shoes," he said. "Some asshole already puked on them."

Rosalyn was standing next to Charlie, her arms crossed aggressively. "Had enough to drink yet, Dora?" she asked.

"Thish place is gross," I slurred.

"Agreed," said Rosalyn. "Can we go?"

Charlie said, "Can't say I'm impressed with the show. The singers are worse than *American Idol* rejects."

"Stella Walters," called the announcer. "Is there a Stella Walters in the house?"

Her posse cheered. Stella toss-tossed her hair over

her shoulders, giving it volume and bounce, and then sprang onstage with the lean grace of a gazelle. She was magnetic, for sure. But I was still angry about what she said.

To the guitar player—Stephan—she said, "The one we practiced."

He said something to the rest of the band, and they started playing a soft, quiet melody I recognized instantly.

"Be a good girl," sang Stella. "You gotta try a little harder. / That simply wasn't good enough / to make us proud."

It was Alanis Morrissette's "Perfect," a sad song about the impossible demands parents put on their kids. My mom was a huge Alanis fan, like, ten years ago, so I had to listen to the album *Jagged Little Pill* approximately a thousand times in the Volvo on trips out of town. Whenever this song came on, Mom and Dad (the softies) would start bawling, and babble to Joya and me about how they loved us unconditionally, and that they'd never make impossible demands or put undue pressure on us. Joya and I would look at each other and say, "They crazy."

So I had the sentimental association with the song. And my emotions weren't exactly in check, having had three beers, and been slighted by Stella as a worshipful infant. I would've had an emotional experience regardless of her performance. That said,

Stella sang from the heart, as if she were telling the story of her own flawed childhood. During the bridge ("I'm doing this for your own damn good / What's the problem / Why are you crying?"), Stella's eyes shone with tears, giving her face a riveting intensity. It was simply impossible to look away.

The singing? To be objective, meh. My inner Paula Abdul was saying, "Pitchy."

The performance? Fantastic. Miles better than any other singer tonight. When Stella finished, the room was silent for a beat and then erupted in the first genuine applause of the evening.

Charlie said, "Whoa. I have to say, I'm impressed."

I was blown away. Stella's "just a kid" and "she looks up to me" comments were thereby erased from my mind. I stared at her with loyal devotion as she took her bows. I thought, She's my friend. She invited me here. She likes me.

I basked in Stella's reflected glory, dimmed only slightly by grouchy Rosalyn. "Exactly what I expected," she said. "It's the onstage version of how she panders to customers at the restaurant."

I knew what Rosalyn meant, sort of. "You're jealous," I blurted instead. Beer made me blurt, apparently.

Rosalyn thought my retort was funny. It was the first time in weeks of working with her that I'd heard her laugh. "Me, jealous of Stella? Couldn't be farther from the truth."

"I don't believe you," I said. "Look at her!"

Stella had climbed offstage and was engulfed by her friends and admirers. They were hugging her, congratulating her. It was an orgy of love and adoration.

I might've salivated from the sight, like a starving person would over grilling meat. Then Rosalyn grabbed my chin and turned my face away from Stella. "Look at me, Dora. Look in my eyes. Am I lying when I say that Stella has nothing, not a single solitary thing, that I want?"

I looked into Rosalyn's caramel brown eyes, and found another version of riveting intensity in there. I guess you could call it Naked Truth. When Rosalyn was sure she had my complete attention, when it felt like we were the only two people in the room, she said, "My dreams are much, much bigger than this shit hole." She dropped my chin, recrossed her arms, and looked away.

I swallowed hard. The noise started filtering back into my head, and I felt the sticky, beery air on my arms and back.

Charlie said, "Incoming."

Stella was upon us. She encircled the Brick crew in a tight hug. "I'm winning!" said the singer, flush with triumph. "I'm going to get the solo gig. I can feel it!" Then she floated back to her table.

Charlie said, "I'm ready to go, if you guys are."

"Beyond ready," said Rosalyn, already walking out.

9

I thought I knew what a hangover was. I thought wrong. When I woke up the next morning, a punishing throb reverberated in my skull. My stomach churned. My skin was gray as ash. This was why I should avoid alcohol at all costs—even under threat of death, which was exactly what this hangover felt like. I could blame only myself. No one put a gun to my head and said, "Drink this beer or the kid gets it."

Just a kid. Stella's comment came rushing back to me, and made my head hurt more.

I tried to go back to sleep—it'd taken me hours to doze off last night, owing to my beer-related insomnia—but couldn't. It was supposed to be my sleep-in Saturday. Jorge was so pleased I got Rosalyn to go out that he gave me the day off. Not as kind as it sounded: Jorge wasn't expecting to serve more than a couple dozen tables, if that, on the holiday weekend. He didn't need me around anyway.

I wondered what Noel and his dad did last night. If they'd watched fireworks in some sleepy New England town, or were alone on a mountaintop, skinning possum for a stew. It would've been nice to go up on our roof, just me and Noel, oohing and ahing about the explosions in the air, and the ones we made ourselves.

Imagining fireworks only increased the pounding in my head. If Noel called, I'd feel better. His voice would be a tonic. His words of love would settle my stomach. Ring, damn phone!

A silent rebuke from the phone on my desk. Mocked by a piece of plastic.

I crawled out of bed and dug in my purse on the floor for my cell. Two bars, one message. From Stella, at one in the morning, asking why I left Magna Mango so early, and that she won the open mike.

Yippee for her.

Scrolling through my contact list, I found the number I needed and hit SEND. The phone rang three times, and a woman picked up.

"Hello?" she asked.

Hearing her voice, I instantly regretted succumbing to impulse. It wasn't exactly drunk dialing. Postdrunk dialing?

"Hello?" she repeated.

"Ms. Kepner," I addressed Noel's mom. "It's Dora Benet. Sorry if I woke you."

"It's nearly noon, Dora," she said, her voice bouncy and alert.

"Yeah. Uh, how's it going?"

"Very well," she said. "And you?"

"Oh, swell. Just great," I said. "I was calling to say hi. And, er, to ask if you'd heard from Noel and Mr. Kepner."

Pause. Lengthening. Uncomfortably. "Hold on a minute, Dora," she said, and I heard muffled conversation. Dear God, was she "entertaining" an overnight guest?

"Of course I've heard from them," she said. "They've checked in a few times."

As glad as I was to learn Noel was okay, the news that he'd checked in with her depressed the hell out of me. "That's fantastic," I said.

"Noel hasn't called you?" she asked, with enough concern to deeply embarrass me.

"Sure!" I lied. "Just not in a few days."

"They've been in and out of cell phone range," she said. "I'm sure Noel will give you a ring again very soon."

We hung up. She, no doubt, returned to her Match.com date, already in progress. She might be having orgies every night in that house since Noel took off. She was probably happy he was gone. And me? Beyond not.

I hated this. Hated! The deadening silence from

Noel was driving me to drink! He *had* forgotten about me. Maybe the best thing I could do for myself was to forget about him.

And the only way to do that was to hook up with a new guy.

Chirp. Cell. It rang in my hand. I was so startled, I dropped the phone and had to lean down to pick it up, which made the blood in my head slam against my brainpan. I nearly passed out from dizziness.

I managed to flip open the phone and blurt, "Noel?"

"Is this the number for Adora Benet?"

Not Noel. "Who's calling?" I asked.

"Zack Gerritson from the Friends Animal Center on Atlantic Avenue."

Huh? Who? "The guy in the white coat? Young-ish, brown hair, tall?"

"I suppose," he said.

Oh yeah, I remembered him. The drool-worthy vet I'd seen in the window of the animal shelter the day I handed out resumes. "You're a vet?" I asked.

"Yup," he said.

"Does that make you a V.D.? Cause that's kind of sad. For your whole profession, I mean."

"It's D.V.M., doctor of veterinary medicine," he said. "Semitransposed D.M.V., department of motor vehicles."

Better than V.D. "This is Dora," I said.

"About a month ago, you filled out a job application at Friends," he said.

I could hear faint barking in the background. "I thought you were hired up."

"Unfortunately, we had a couple of no-shows and dropouts," he said. "And the last kid we hired quit to go away for the weekend. Look, Ms. Benet, I've been alone here for twenty hours, and I've got a lot of animals in need of attention. I'm at my wit's end. Are you still interested in a job? If so, can you come in today? I'll pay you."

So much for the reliability of people who planned ahead. And who gets called to fly in to the rescue? Me, the last-minuter. I was flattered, but also still flattened. The throbbing in my temple beat out the Morse code for "no stinking way am I going to listen to barking dogs all day long." But I pictured the face of the hot doc, looking sad and alone. How grateful he'd be when I walked through the door to hear the soft purr of kittens and feel the nuzzling of puppies.

"What's the going rate?" I had to ask.

He told me. It was pathetic. No wonder all those other hires bailed.

"What would you have me do?" I asked.

"Clean out cages, feed and water the animals. Groom the dogs. Assist me in the examination room. Nothing complicated. I just need an extra pair of hands."

I looked at my hands, still a bit shaky. I'd heard of "hair of the dog" hangover cures. Somehow, I didn't think that had to do with actual dog hair.

"When do you need me?" I asked. A shower, some food, and I'd be good to go in a few hours.

"Now?" he asked. "Please, Ms. Benet. You're the only person on file who answered the phone. I'll pay double. Triple."

He was desperate. Exactly how I liked my men. If a girl came off that needy, a guy would run screaming for the hills. But Zack's neediness hit me in the tender spot. The nurturing impulse in my female genes kicked in.

"I'm on the way," I said, like Supergirl.

I'd remembered Zack as handsome. But I hadn't remembered him as smoking *hot*. This sexy should be illegal. It might actually be a crime in several states. Tall, slim but sinewy, close-cropped brown hair that showcased his perfectly shaped head, those flashing green eyes I'd noticed through a pane of glass. He had some scruff. Not obnoxiously purposeful; I think he'd been too busy to shave. He smelled like dog shampoo.

"Ms. Benet?" he asked when I walked in the animal center door.

"Dora. I'm ready to scoop poop," I said.

"I'm in your debt," he said, clasping my hands, his green eyes burning into my hazel ones.

"Do I call you Dr. Gerritson?"

"No one calls me Dr. Gerritson. That makes me sound ancient. Zack, please."

"How old are you?" I had to ask.

"Twenty-seven," he said. "Let's get right to work, okay?"

Zack brought me to the wall of caged cats. From the street, the boxes were deceptively small. Up close, I could see that each cat had adequate space, a soft towel to sleep on, food and water dishes, and a toy to play with. The compartments also had a carpeted tube to climb on or crawl into. Most of the cats were hiding behind or inside their cubby.

"Okay, that's too cute," I said, pointing at a snowy white kitten curled into a ball in the back of its cage. The name on the cage door said ANGEL.

Zack nodded. "Angel's already been adopted. Five families were vying for her. Rocky, over here, has been living in the showcase wall for months."

"No takers?" I stooped down to peer into Rocky's compartment. He was a large, orange, fully grown cat, kind of fat, with a short tail, a tattered ear and a scar on his cheek. When I said, "Hello, Rocky," in a very pleasant tone, the animal hissed at me and tried to claw me through the cage door.

I jerked back, nearly falling on my ass. "I think Rocky might feel more at home in an asylum," I said. "Or in the wild."

"We found him in the wild," said Zack. "The wild of Bensonhurst. He'd been used as a target in a game of darts by a bunch of kids. It's no wonder he hates people. People have caused him nothing but pain."

The expression on Zack's face! It was gloriously emotional and heartfelt. I almost cried, not only for Rocky's horrible life, but by how affected Zack was by it. This man had a heart of melty golden butter.

"Are you the only vet here?" I asked.

"Me and two others work in shifts," he said. "This summer, I'm pretty much in charge, though. And there's Donna Snagg, of course. You probably met her when you filled out the application."

I remembered the nega-blonde in the lab coat. "Where is she today?"

"On a much-deserved vacation," he said. "This way to the courtyard. We have a few dog runs set up behind the building."

I followed him down the corridor. He had a saucy butt. I was glad he wasn't wearing the long white coat today. Along the way, I noticed the corridor's pastel pink walls, the posters of dogs and cats (HANG IN THERE, KITTY!). The cheerful vibe lightened my hangover considerably. My mood was improved, too.

I hadn't thought about Noel since I arrived. Until now, by realizing I hadn't.

We passed exam rooms with stainless steel tables, cabinets full of medical supplies, animal scales and a large basin in each. At the end of the corridor, Zack opened the back door to the building's courtyard. Unlike most brownstone gardens, this one wasn't artfully landscaped with flowering plants. It held two large dog runs and a footpath between them.

Inside each cage were—surprise!—dogs. Six total. I recognized some breeds. A Lab. Some kind of terrier. The rest were pit bulls.

"We rescue the pit bulls from all over Brooklyn," he said. "People get them for protection, and then they don't make the effort to properly train them. The dogs are difficult to control untrained, so the owners set them loose in parks or on the street."

"Are they going to bite my hand off?" I asked, backing away.

"Pit bulls have the reputation of being aggressive, but if they're well trained, they're gentle and affectionate."

A lot of boys were like that, too.

"So you're saying these pit bulls have been trained?"

He nodded. "Painstakingly, by me and the other vets."

"Emphasis on 'pain'?" I asked.

Zack frowned. "Would you describe yourself as a compassionate person, Dora?"

"I have a finely developed sense of guilt," I said. "Which, from certain points of view, looks a lot like compassion. And I've been working on my empathy skills all year long."

"Try to see through the dog's eyes," he suggested. "If you treat them well, they'll like you. I wouldn't send you in there if I thought for a second that you were in danger."

"Send me in there?" I asked.

He pointed into one of the cages. "See that shovel?"

"Yes," I said.

"See the piles?"

I saw them, and boy did I *smell* them.

He said, "Dump into the receptacles in the corner there. The kibble and hose are over there. Refill the food and water. Then come back inside and I'll teach you how to check a cat for ear mites."

He went back inside. I gulped, and began my tasks. Imagine, having existed on this planet for seventeen years and somehow avoiding shoveling shit. How had my parents steered me so far from this unrivaled pungent adventure? It was a humbling, stinky business, enhanced by the acrid tang of terror about being caged with formerly ferocious beasts.

I probably would have quit on the spot, but I didn't want to disappoint Zack.

One dog, the biggest pit bull, with a brown mug and pointy ears, took a particular interest in me—or, I should say, in my leg. Another cowered in the corner, as if I were going to attack him (her?) with the shovel, which convinced me that, at any second, the dog would overcome its fear and make a lunge for my throat.

Funny to discover that I had a fear of dogs. I'd walked among them—Brooklyn Heights was a dog lover's paradise—my whole life, and never felt the slightest twinge. But those dogs were on leashes, walked by owners who were quick to describe the animal as "friendly" or "cranky." I'd spent a good amount of time with my grandparents' dogs and been fine. But out here, in the cage, I was alone with approximately four hundred pounds of canine teeth and muscle—and shaking in my flip-flops.

When I finished the cleanup and feeding, I ran back inside the building and breathed deeply until the fear dissipated.

Zack heard me come in, and called me into the exam room, where he was giving the once-over to Angel the kitten.

"From now on, I'd prefer working only with cats," I said.

He squinted at me. "Did they growl?"

"No," I said quickly. "They were good. I, er, wasn't entirely relaxed."

Zack nodded. He didn't press the point, bless his melty-butter heart. Like his animal friends, he probably sensed my fear. "We've got more than enough for you to do with just cats, okay?"

"Thank you," I said, relieved.

"Now hold Angel like this while I collect a stool sample," he said.

"How do you do that?" I asked, placing my hands on the furry creature on the table.

"With this." He held up a long plastic stick with a tiny spoonlike tip. "Get a good grip on her," he said. "I'm going in."

10

"You haven't lived until you've seen cat shit under a microscope," I told Dad that night. "It's a metropolis of germs and worms and parasites."

Mom said, "You should write a college application essay about that."

I couldn't tell if she was serious. "Yeah, I could say how scooping fecal matter from the rear end of an animal is a metaphor for the war in Iraq."

Dad lowered his newspaper. "Is it?"

I shrugged. "Probably."

Mom was flipping channels with the sound off, searching for something to commit to. "Tell us about the vet."

How dreamy he was? How, when we stood shoulder to shoulder over the microscope, I shivered? How our eyes met over the kitty litter box, and lingered while we sifted for solid waste?

"Zack Gerritson, D.V.M.," I said. "He's from Brooklyn, grew up in Cobble Hill in the 1990s."

"How old is he?" asked Mom, her eyes off the TV and on me.

"I think he said late twenties."

Mom had a sixth sense. It told her whenever I was lying. She raised her well-plucked eyebrows and asked, "What's he look like?"

Shrugged again. "He's tallish. Average. He's not the dog's dinner to look at. But nothing special."

"Really," said Mom, smiling thinly.

I had a sixth sense, too. I could see dread, people. A thick coating of it was all over Mom. What was she worried about? That I'd fall in love with a gorgeous veterinarian who was old enough to be my much older brother?

Dad said, "Ever heard the expression 'When the cat's away, the mice will play'?"

"Who's the cat in your equation?" I asked. "Is Noel the cat? And I'm the helpless mouse who lives in constant fear for my life?"

"Just saying," Dad just said.

"*I'm* the cat," I said.

"Noel lives in constant fear?" asked Mom.

"No one is the cat or the mouse," I said. "And honestly, I've reached my limit of animal references for one day."

"So tell me more about this vet," said Mom.

"Let me ask you two something," I redirected. "Why is it that we never had any pets growing up?

Liza had a cat for years. Even Eli had a hamster, until it gnawed off its own leg and was too grotesque to keep around."

Dad said, "Gloria and I decided that four defecating mammals in one apartment was quite enough."

"I can understand that while Joya and I were in diapers," I said. "But what about after? We begged."

"Dogs smell," said Mom. "Have you ever been stuck in a room with a wet dog? It's nauseating. And they get hair all over the furniture. Cats are even worse. They leave tufts of fur on everything. Male cats pee on the walls. And, half the time, cats hate their owners anyway. You give and give, and get nothing back."

"Minor inconveniences compared to the magical bond between a girl and her pet," I said.

"I grew up with dogs," said Dad, as if I didn't know. His parents, my grandparents, were insane dog people. They had three black Labs, and treated Moe, Larry and Curly like human children, with their full schedule of play groups, exercise classes, doctor's and grooming appointments. Gram and Gramp fed them in bowls at the table, and let them sleep in their bed. The Stooges had clothing custom made for the winter months, including fitted hoodies and booties that were sickeningly cute. There were more pictures of the Stooges—and other, dead dogs of the past—around Gram and Gramp's house than of Dad and us, or my uncle Sam and the cousins. "From my perspective," Dad continued, "there's something masochistic about opening your heart to a creature whose lifespan is significantly shorter than your own."

"You mean when the pet dies," I said.

Dad nodded. "It's rough, especially for kids."

"I'm not a kid," I said, still bristling from Stella's comment.

"But you were when you wanted a pet," said Mom.

"I still want one," I said, a bit shrilly.

Mom frowned. "Where is this coming from?"

"You're going to college in a year," said Dad. "Makes no sense to get a pet now."

A pet wasn't good for me back then, and it made no sense now. I started to feel condescended to, treated like a helpless, vulnerable creature who couldn't take care of herself. Like I was their human pet.

"I thought that with Joya away, the three of us would form a new understanding of trust and respect."

"Why would you think *that*?" asked Dad, grinning.

"You see?" I said. "You discount my opinions."

Mom sighed. "Can't we just stare mindlessly at the TV like normal people?"

"I'm not taken seriously!" I said. "You don't think I'm responsible enough to take care of a cat. I am. And when I go to college, I'll take it with me." I pictured Angel in my arms, introducing her to my college roommate, whomever she was, at whatever school I went to. We'd bond over Angel's white fluffy cuddliness. Everyone would want to pet Angel for good luck before tests, and I'd be the most popular girl in the dorm.

Dad squinted at me. He seemed to be seeing me with a new perspective, as if I were a force to be reckoned with, finally. He opened his mouth, and I thought for a thrilling, frightening moment he was going to agree to all my demands. But then my cell started to chirp.

Mom said, "Why don't you take that in your room?"

"This conversation is not over," I said, heading up the stairs to my room and flipping open my phone.

"Hello?"

"Meet me at Shin Ju in ten minutes," said Stella breathlessly. "It's important!"

"What's the matter?" I asked, alarmed by her urgency.

"I'm hungry, that's what!"

I laughed. It was after nine. I'd already eaten with Mom and Dad. And it was a bit late, with the morning shift at the Brick. And I was tired after sifting through feline stool all day. But when Stella called, people jumped.

"Okay, order a tempura roll for me," I said.

"Zack sounds hot," said Stella at the bar at Shin Ju half an hour later. "A sexy older doctor. Sort of. He might be exactly what you need this summer, Dora."

"Well, I'm getting a major dose," I said. "I'm going to work every Saturday at the animal center."

"Sounds excellent," she said. "Except that's one less shift we'll be working together at the Brick."

Stella had been great tonight, letting me do all the talking from the minute I sat down next to her at the sushi bar. She hadn't brought up last night, her glory at Magna Mango, the five guys who probably locked antlers over who got to take her home.

Which gave me pause (but only after I'd talked myself breathless). "I've been totally dominating," I said. "Tell me what happened after I left last night."

She nodded. "Well, I won. A couple of guys got stupid at the end of the night, so I ditched them both."

"You don't seem too excited about winning," I said.

She signaled for the sushi chef and ordered more sake. Her second carafe. I'd sampled the first. The rice wine was served hot, to be drunk out of tiny porcelain cups that looked like overgrown thimbles. The sake was flavorless, but it warmed my throat all the way down. The sensation lingered for almost a minute. I liked it.

While the chef replenished her carafe, Stella said, "I'm happy, believe me. Every win helps. But singing in a dump like Magna Mango is not what I want."

I thought about Rosalyn saying *My dreams are bigger than this shit hole*. Stella's dreams were, too.

"And I kind of felt bad about you, actually," added Stella softly.

"Me?" I asked, surprised.

"I got the impression you were pissed at me when you left."

I stammered, "No! I was just tired. And confused."

"You weren't mad I told Brad you were just a kid?"

Brad? "Oh, you mean Brian."

"Who's Brian?"

"I wasn't pissed. I was grateful you told him to leave me alone," I said.

"Okay," she said, nodding suspiciously. "But for the record, I don't think of you as a kid. I only said that to make Brad disgusted with himself for groping you. You're way more evolved than I was at your age. Two jobs? You hardly drink, you don't smoke. You're faithful to your boyfriend, even when he doesn't call you."

Ouch. Like I needed the reminder.

"The summer before my senior year," she continued, "I lived in a house on Fire Island with ten other kids from St. Andrew's. I screwed around, spent money like water, partied every night. It ended in the worst way when my parents got their Visa bill, and came out to the island to take me home."

"Nightmare," I said, pitying her for that humiliation.

"No shit," she replied. "It was horrible. But, as you can see, I've come a long way since then." Stella lifted her thimble of sake and then downed it. "I think you're a good influence on me, if you wanna know." When the sushi chef was at the other end of the bar, she grabbed another sake cup from the stack. "Let's toast to being good influences on each other."

She filled my thimble. It was so little liquid. No more than one or two ounces. How could a baby-sized portion have any effect? You'd have to drink a hundred of these cups to equal the alcohol content of a single beer.

I held my cup aloft and said, "Skoal."

We drank.

Stella poured again. "'Cause I mean it, Dora. I see something special in you. I recognized it that first day at the Brick. How you held it together despite all those mistakes! You were hilarious, begging at the customers to have you fired. I thought, 'Get to know this girl.' "

I was flattered, surprised, bashful. I wondered if it was the sake. Deciding to retain my usual cynical optimism, I took Stella's assessment at face value. She saw something extraordinary about me. Who was I to object?

"I was drawn to you, too, at first sight," I said, the words tumbling out on their own. "You must be aware, Stella, that you're magnetic. A gravitational force. Have you *ever* walked into a room and not been the center of attention?"

That made her explode with laughter. "Oh, Dora," she said, a fluttery hand on her breastbone. "You have NO idea."

I guess I didn't. She kept chortling at high volume. I was self-conscious, but also enthralled to have made her laugh.

"Another toast," she said. "To our mutual appreciation society!"

"Cheers!" I said, and we drank.

"I really do think you're very talented," I said. "Seeing you on stage. The raw emotion. You looked like you were really feeling it. Serious anguish."

"What about the singing?" she asked.

Mediocre at best. But with the technology available, the prickly edges of her tone could be sanded away. What mattered was presence, and she had it. But she didn't need to hear a critique from me.

"The singing was AWESOME!" I might've been yelling. "I was BLOWN AWAY. You were born to sing, you realize this. You must sing, and share your gift with the world!"

She grabbed my wrists. "I feel exactly the same way. When I sing, I can feel the power of the universe. Like I'm surfing the cosmos. Not that I've ever gone surfing. But it's the *feeling*, you know?"

I tried to imagine what the hell she was talking about. The universe and the cosmos were places I ceded to Joya and Liza, who dwelled in ethereal realms. Eli and I were citizens of Brooklyn, New York. When Joya rambled about visible auras and harmonic convergence, I rolled my eyes and grumbled. Something about Stella, though, made me want to believe (1) that the astral plane did exist, and (2) that she could sing her way onto it.

"What's it feel like?" I asked, eyes wide, the sake-soaked portion of my brain expanding inside my skull. "Being onstage?"

Stella moaned loudly, as if she were reliving the glorious sensation. A few other customers looked over at us. "It's an *incredible* feeling," she said, again, a mite too passionately for a public place. "It's better than *drugs*, *booze*, SEX. It's five thousand orgasms at the same time!"

Okay, now every person in the restaurant was looking at her, including the chefs and waitresses who barely spoke English.

Five thousand orgasms, eh? That would be quite the thrill. I was amazed by just one.

"Sounds intense," I said.

"And almost painful," she enthused. "But it's a good pain. Hurts so good. The kind of pain I want to feel again and again and again." She fixed her eyes on me. I could tell they weren't exactly focused. My vision had gone wonky, too.

She put her hand on my knee, got serious for a second. "Dora, I'm going to tell you something I've never told another soul," said Stella.

"Are you sure?" I asked. Interestingly enough, I'd been told big secrets by unlikely sources before. From people who, like Stella, barely knew me, and/ or would ordinarily have little to say to me. I thought immediately of Sondra Fortune, my sworn enemy, Ruling Class queen at Brownstone. She'd confided in me during a time of extreme emotional upheaval in her life. She was as shocked as I was, to have made me the keeper of her secrets.

Stella drew a deep breath and said, "I want to die onstage."

I pictured her on the low rise at Magna Mango, amid the grime and sticky beer cups, the acrid aroma of too many bodies in too small a space, Stella hitting a high note and then collapsing, the microphone still clutched in her hand.

She said, "Can't you see it?"

Unfortunately, yes. "Totally," I said.

"This is how I see it," she said, painting her vision. "I'm much older than I am now. I've been a superstar, like Madonna, for decades. I'm a household name. Starving children in Africa know who I am and can sing my tunes. I'm performing at a big concert to benefit world peace. The president and heads of state from all over the world have come for this historic event. I'm wearing a cobalt blue sequined dress, my makeup and hair are perfection. Between songs, I make a plea that the nations of the world join together in love and harmony, to fight greenhouse emissions and feed the poor. Then my band begins playing one of my biggest hits, a poignant song, slow and sad, but ultimately optimistic. I start to sing. People in the audience feel the power. They're overwhelmed, start to cry, and swear to each other that war is over. They send me wave after wave of love, and I take it in. It surrounds me and sinks into my skin, and then my heart literally explodes from all that love."

Stella stopped there. Her breath was short. She panted lightly. I wondered how many times she'd played this scene in her head, each time adding a few details, until the picture was as clear as if she were watching it in high def. She really believed this would actually happen.

Rosalyn had said that her dreams were bigger than a dive bar in the East Village. If Rosalyn only knew: Stella had some pretty immense dreams, too. I was impressed. A bit wigged out, wondering if Stella was delusional. But impressed, nonetheless.

I said, "Another toast."

She raised her sake cup.

"To a purposeful life," I said, "which doesn't necessarily mean finding religion."

"I'll drink to that!" sang Stella.

We drank and then started giggling. Which grew into a chuckle. Then a guffaw, and finally into all-out paroxysms of laughter, tears streaming, diaphragms leaping.

It was at that moment, when I was doubled over, snorting and practically foaming at the mouth, that someone tapped me on the shoulder and said, "Adora Benet, what exactly do you think you're doing?"

My bones chilled. I knew that voice. Turning, cringing, I said, "Oh. No."

Anita Stomp. Eli's mother, the bites-heads-off-of-tough-guys-and-spits-them-out litigator for one of the biggest law firms in Manhattan. The woman who could kill with her Death Stare. She could drop you with one eye tied behind her back.

"Hello, Dora!" said her cheerful husband, Bertram,

a retired family physician, my former pediatrician, and the only man, besides my father and Noel, who'd seen me naked. "Having a good time?"

"Yes, thanks for asking," I said meekly.

Mrs. Stomp leaned closer, sniffed aggressively. "You've been drinking. You're underage. This restaurant could be closed down by the police for serving a minor. Do you want to be responsible for depriving the residents of this neighborhood from their favorite sushi bar, just so you and your friend can be loud, offensive and an embarrassment to yourself and everyone who knows you?"

"No, ma'am," I said.

"Then you'd better get out of here, before the police arrive and find you in this state." Anita fixed her lethal gaze at Stella. "And you are?"

"Stella Walters," she said, all sweetness and smiles. She was either immune to Anita Stomp's intimidating mojo, or Stella was a better actor than she was a singer.

"Are you a minor?" asked Anita.

"Are you my mother?" asked Stella.

Anita Stomp flinched. So did I. Stella would never have to see the Stomps again. But I would pay for my friend's lip many times over. Anita grinned savagely, probably writing in her head the statement she planned to deliver to my parents later tonight.

"Good night, Adora," said Anita. "I'm sure we'll see you very soon."

Bertram shot me a sympathetic glance as they walked out of Shin Ju. He was a kind, supportive softy. I took his sympathy for what it was worth. Probably not much, once my parents got Anita's report.

The idea of that sobered me up quick.

Stella, too, seemed deflated.

"I'd better get home," I said, pulling a couple of twenties from my wallet. "Early shift at the Brick tomorrow."

"I'll see you there," she said.

We paid and left. Stella and I walked part of the way home, but the happy vibe of the evening had been punctured by the Stomps. Plus, there was the anticipatory anxiety. Something terrible awaited me at home. The reproachful scowls of my parents. The cold look of their disappointment.

But when I finally got to our building and climbed the stairs to our apartment, I was greeted upon entry by silence and darkness.

Mom and Dad had gone to bed. On the dining room table, I found a note. Mom's handwriting. It said:

Noel called. He's sorry he missed you.

I nearly cried, reading it. Missing his call was my punishment for behaving badly at Shin Ju. I checked my cell. The battery was dead. Plugging it in, I hoped he'd left a long, rambling message on voice mail about his deep and abiding love for me.

He had left a message. But it was the garbled hum of bad reception. I could barely make out a single word.

Feeling sorry for myself, and knowing that once Mom spoke to Anita Stomp, my self-pity would quadruple, I dragged my sorry (you didn't know how sorry) ass to bed.

While I lay there, I thought about the size of my dreams. I tried to scratch together a vision of my future, an over-the-top fantasy about the way things would be for me. I got only wispy, cloudy flashes.

Of me older, chicer, walking down Montague Street, smiling placidly, holding someone's hand, but I couldn't tell whose.

Of me typing at a laptop—didn't know where—pausing, and then the sudden brightness of a eureka moment hitting me. I bent over the keyboard with renewed vigor, fingers moving at lightning speed.

Of me on the porch swing of a Victorian mansion, same era as the brownstone I lived in now, but this was a freestanding house with a lawn.

I liked all the pictures. But they lacked cohesiveness, a glued-together idea of where I'd be, what I'd be doing, and who I'd do it with. I drifted off, unsure about everything except the relief and reward of deep sleep.

11

July 10, 2008
To: abenet@brownstone.edu
From: estomp@brownstone.edu
Subject: You = In Trouble

This is how it's supposed to work: Two friends share their lives and secrets with each other, often talking about their boyfriends. This is NOT how it's supposed to work: One friend gets all her news about her other friend *from* her boyfriend. Your lazy e-mailing habits have put Charlie in the position of Town Gossip, which he says has made him grow breasts. I don't want a boyfriend with breasts, Dora. I blame you.

Meanwhile, here in the land of wieners and strudel, I've been totally immersed in music. The youth orchestra plays eight hours a day. And then we break into small groups for dinner to talk about music (usually in English). The Austrian people are immune to sarcasm or irony. When they're happy, they're HAPPY.

When they're sad, they're suicidal. The earnestness here is manic-depressive.

Deep confession coming: Before I left Brooklyn, I thought playing and talking about music 24/7 with people who were as good or better than me would be a dream come true. But I'm sorry to say that all music, all the time is kind of boring. There's some romantic intrigue among some kids in the orchestra, but not me, and I don't really care about their flings. I don't care about anyone here. I miss you and Liza, Brooklyn, Charlie, my parents. I'm rethinking a lot, Dora. I always wanted to make piano my life's work. To travel the world, playing for music lovers. But now I'm not so sure. I'm better than most of the other pianists here, but I sense they'll go farther than I will. I've got the fingers but not the heart. I'm beginning to understand an important truth about life. Here it comes. Pay attention.

Success isn't about how good you are; it's about how bad you want it.

July 11, 2008
To: estomp@brownstone.edu
Fro: abenet@brownstone.edu
Re: hopes and dreams

Who says you have to know exactly what you want out of life at seventeen? Where is it written that we have to have a crystal-clear picture of our future when we're not old enough to vote, drink, go to war, rent a car or smoke a cigarette? So you thought you wanted one thing, and now you're changing your mind. That's normal! It's healthy! It's a woman's friggin' prerogative, for fock's sake. It'd be crazy and tragic to force yourself to follow a dream that stops making sense. It's not how good you are, or how bad you want it, but how much you *get* it. Or not. I don't exactly get it (whatever it is) myself.

So Charlie is giving you my updates. Has your mother mentioned me, by any chance? Your parents busted me a few days ago at Shin Ju, all drunk and disorderly. I've been waiting for your mom to tell my mom about it. And waiting. Anita is truly sinister (and I mean that with the utmost respect and admiration). She's torturing me by NOT telling my parents. I'm living with an axe hanging inches over my head, Eli! It's terrifying. And there's a lot at stake here! In a week, Mom and Dad are leaving for Vermont for Joya's parents' weekend at camp, and they're making noises about letting me stay here alone. Otherwise, they'll call in my New Jersey grandma to babysit me like I'm nine.

July 12, 2008
To: abenet@brownstone.edu
Fr: lgreene@brownstone.edu
Re: have you heard from Noel yet?

I'm in love again. His name is Jerome. He's the son of the South Hampton Golf Club pro. His family is from Ireland—big golfers over there, who knew?—but they live full-time in Bermuda. Golf is a year-round sport here, unlike snorkeling. You *could* snorkel in winter here, but the water gets pretty cold, so hardly any tourists come. What was I saying? Oh, yeah: I'm in love again! This is different than Max or Stanley. It's the real thing. Jerome and I spend every day and night together. He's told me a lot about the private school he goes to in South Hampton. It's more expensive than Brownstone (if that's possible), but it's very good. Considered among the best in the world, he says.

July 13, 2008
To: lgreene@brownstone.edu
From: abenet@brownstone.edu
Subject: you punk

I'm happy you're in love. But if you're thinking of staying in South Hampton and not coming back to Brooklyn for senior year, I'll fly down there and kidnap you. I mean it. The idea of you not coming back to Brownstone is making me cry. My keyboard is all wet.

July 14, 2008
To: abenet@brownstone.edu
From: lgreene@brownstone.edu
Re: Do Not Tell Eli!!!

Okay, yes, I am thinking about living with my parents instead of mooching off my best friend's family for another year. Is that so wrong? And it's not because of Jerome. Not only. I mean, he is a major factor. And Bermuda is paradise, Dora! If you had the opportunity to live here, wouldn't you?

And you better not tell Eli. I'm going to write her a long e-mail about Jerome and South Hampton Academy. But I'm not ready yet. I haven't even hashed out the details with my parents. It's all so exciting!

July 15, 2008
To: lgreene@brownstone.edu
From: abenet@brownstone.edu
Re: speechless

One woman's paradise is another woman's HELL. I don't care how many palm trees grow in Bermuda. If it's not Brooklyn, it ain't happening. How quickly you forget that Brooklyn Heights is the greatest place on earth. And, as of this week, we have a Garden of Eden supermarket, catering to all your organic gourmet shopping needs. Where are you going to find organic kumquats in Bermuda?

July 16, 2008
To: abenet@brownstone.edu
From: lgreene@brownstone.edu
Re: re: speechless

Where to find organic kumquats in Bermuda? Uh, how about *kumquat trees*? They grow all over the island. BTW, this is my last e-mail for a while. We're expecting a big group of tourists from Iowa. I'll have a lot of work to do. Again, DO NOT TELL ELI about Jerome and South Hampton Academy. Meanwhile, you didn't mention Noel. I'll assume he called, you talked, and are as madly in love as I am!

[POSTCARD STUCK ON FRIDGE WITH A MAGNET. ON ONE SIDE, A PHOTO OF A FAMILY OF DEER, A BUCK WITH ANTLERS, A DOE, AND TWO FAWNS. ON THE FLIP SIDE, A HAND-SCRAWLED MESSAGE.]

I can't wait to see you guys! Only a week before you come up for parents' weekend! I've got SO MUCH to show you. My owl sculpture is the talk of camp. The director wants to enter it in a Vermont folk art exhibition. She thinks I can actually SELL it for THOUSANDS OF DOLLARS! Thank you, thank you, thank you for letting me go to art camp. This has been the best summer ever! Love, Joya. P.S. Is Dora coming for visitation weekend? I really, really hope she does.

"Yup, you've come to the right place! It's Noel's voice mail! And you should really leave a message, as soon as you hear the . . . *BEEEEP!*"

"Do I need to identify myself? Maybe I do. Maybe you've forgotten the sound of my voice. So, yeah, it's Dora. I'd say sorry I missed your calls, but there was only that one garbled message I didn't catch a word of. I've decided to assume you said all the right things, including an apology for not calling sooner— or since. I'm working at an animal shelter, by the way. Elbow deep in dog shit. I'll say good-bye now. Good-bye."

12

"I left two hundred dollars in an envelope on the kitchen counter," said Dad. "The fridge is full. If you run out, just order from FreshDirect. My password is dorajoya. One word."

"Okay, that is the most obvious password in the world," I said. "Anyone could crack that."

"This is a mistake," said Mom. "We shouldn't leave her alone."

I sighed heavily. "I'll be fine, Mom. Jeez. Just leave already."

"We really should hit the road, Gloria," said Dad. "Traffic in Connecticut will be murder."

He hugged me and whispered, "Please don't burn the house down."

Then he let me go. Set me free. I walked into Mom's arms next. She was three inches shorter than I, and my arms wrapped around her double. She hugged me as tight as she could (what a weakling!). Her body started shaking, and I realized with horror that she was crying.

I stepped back. Mom was not a crybaby. She rarely got weepy, except in moments of familial bonding and/or separation, as such.

"Get a grip, Mom," I said. "It's only a week."

When my parents finally decided to go to Vermont without me, and leave me by myself in Brooklyn, I rejoiced—privately. I had to keep my unbridled joy tethered, though, or Mom and Dad might think I was planning on throwing a massive party. Instead of hooting like I wanted to, I shrugged and said, "If you're sure . . ."

Underplaying it worked. Dad mapped out a covered-bridge driving tour of New England to follow the weekend camp visit, extending their trip by FIVE WHOLE DAYS. That news nearly shattered my composure. I'd maintained it for about as long as I could. If they didn't leave in the next five minutes, I might blow.

"I'm sorry," said Mom, wiping at her tears. "This is a big step, Dora. You don't realize what this means, do you?"

That they trusted me not to starve to death with a fridge full of food?

"I think I do," I said.

"Do you realize what this means *to me*?" asked Mom.

"That you're old?"

That dried up her tears but quick. "Let's go," she said to Dad, emotional moment over.

"Love to Joya?" asked Dad.

"Sure, why not?" I said.

We hugged and kissed again at the door, and then I forcefully shoved them out. I watched from the kitchen window as they got in the Volvo and drove up Garden Place and out of sight.

That moment was my first real taste of total independence. I savored it. Seriously, I salivated. Drooled, even.

Having a wild party wasn't on my mind. First of all, who would come? My friends were gone! Truthfully, I wasn't sure what I'd do with my time. Go to my jobs. Hang out with Stella at the floating pool. Maybe have her and Rosalyn over. Perhaps invite Zack Gerritson for a candlelit dinner, and then ravage him until he begged for mercy.

Even if that were remotely possible (not), I probably wouldn't be able to go through with it. I wasn't a cheater by nature. Still, Noel's silence did create a vacuum in my fantasy life, which sucked Zack Gerritson to the forefront of my mind. I'd only worked one Saturday so far. I barely knew the guy. And yet the idea of spending time, as an independent woman, at his side filled my veins with rocket fuel. I simply could not wait to see him again.

I gave it another ten minutes, just to be sure Mom and Dad didn't circle around and come back.

Then I took off all my clothes and walked around

the apartment naked. I sat on the couch naked.
I made a sandwich in the kitchen naked. I walked
around the dining room, eating it, bare-assed naked.

I had to do something to claim the space for my
very own. I proceeded upstairs, went into each room,
turned a full circle, as if showing the walls and furniture my junk, marking my territory.

Then I got dressed. I had to get to the Brick for
my shift. In exchange for Saturdays off, I had to work
a double shift on Friday. This was how real life went.
You got up, ate breakfast, went to work, came home
later, made dinner, watched TV and went to bed,
ideally, with someone who made the grind of the day
worth it for the grind of the nights.

If Noel were in Brooklyn, we would be playing
house.

I was hit, suddenly, with a wave of missing him
and the fear that he really had found some Yankee ho
to replace me. This was followed by a wave of loneliness, and the strange hum of an empty house that
wouldn't be filled again for seven long days.

"You're being pathetic," I said aloud. Only an
hour, and I was talking to myself.

The Brick kitchen was bustling when I got there.
Rosalyn was chopping. Ramon and Raul were
frying. Jorge sweated profusely and paced nervously. Charlie was setting tables. I jumped into

the whirlwind, replenishing sugar packets and the silverware bins.

"Where's Stella?" I asked.

"Missing in action," said Jorge.

It was almost ten o'clock when she finally showed up, an hour and a half late. She waved off explaining herself, tied on an apron, and started waiting tables. Privately, by the pantry, she said to me, "Insomnia."

"I get it, too," I said.

"Always when I'm alone in the apartment," she said.

Tonight I'd be alone. I almost asked Stella to sleep over, but I resisted the urge. How lame would it be if I couldn't last a single night by myself?

Jorge yelled, "Come on, people! Get out there and move bacon!"

We got out there. Moved bacon. Also sausage, eggs, pancakes, waffles, home fries and toast. Loaves and loaves of toast. Occasionally, Stella would reset my tables, Rosalyn would plate my food when I got overwhelmed. But I could tell by Jorge's relatively dry forehead that I was improving. I hadn't dumped anything on anyone in weeks, but the morning was young.

Out of the corner of my eyes, I noticed a new customer was sitting down at an uncleared table. I rushed over and started piling up the dirty plates, not even looking at the guest. I said, "Just let me get rid of this and I'll be right back to . . ."

"Fringe Girl?"

I froze, midclearing. Swallowing hard, I looked up, into the face of my customer. "Sondra," I said, fake smiling at the exotic face of my sworn enemy. Well, make that sworn frenemy. I loathed her ruthlessness, for sure. But we had shared some moments—and boyfriends. She wasn't *all* bad. Only 97 percent evil.

Even in tennis gear, Sondra looked glamorous. White fabric looked excellent against her dark skin. She accessorized the polo shirt and skort with gold bangles and hoop earrings. Full makeup, on a steaming-hot day, to hit a ball. And me, in tight black chinos, a stained white shirt, and a grease-splattered apron. My hair was droopy from the kitchen heat. My only makeup was a thin coating of shine from working hard. I could never compete with Sondra in the looks (popularity, money, connections, etc.) department(s), but I liked to think I had her beat in terms of emotional fortitude.

"Fringe, I had no idea," she said, grinning with demonic precision. "I thought you took some save-the-world gardening job."

"I thought waitressing would be a better way to fully understand the complexities of my social democracy," I said. "I'm in search of awareness, Sondra. Which is, of course, of no interest to you."

"You got that right," she said. "Good luck with

your awareness," said Sondra, her green eyes flashing. "I can help, if you'd like. People can rarely see
in themselves what others see clearly in five seconds.
So if you're searching for personal insight, I can give
you a shove in the right direction."

I was sure she'd love to. "Are you working this
summer?" I asked. "Or just sponging?"

"I'm interning at *Project Runway*," she said.

The dream job. I bit my lip, kept myself from gush-
ing about Heidi Klum and Tim Gunn. "That sounds
perfect for you. Stylish, and short on substance."

"And your job, ideal for you," she purred. "Gritty.
And humble."

"You're eating alone this morning?" I asked.

"Oh, here he is," she said, her eyes going to the
dining room entrance.

Stanley Nable. Sondra's boyfriend. Formerly Liza's
boyfriend. He dumped Liza, then hooked up with
Sondra with suspicious alacrity. Stanley denied starting to see Sondra until after he and Liza were officially over. Stanley was a solid, honest guy; had
always been emotionally sincere. Ordinarily, I'd have
believed him.

But since the girl was Sondra, and Liza was my
best friend, I was beholden to hate him on principle,
and have nothing to do with him. Which wasn't easy.
Stanley was Noel's best friend.

"Dora!" he said when he got over to the table. He

wrapped me in a tight bear hug. "How's your summer been?"

I forgot for a second that I loathed him. "You look awesome," I said. He really did. His cocoa skin was richer than ever, and his hair, usually shorn, was growing into a cool mini 'fro.

Sondra said, "You like his hair, Fringe? My doing."

Hearing "Fringe" again made me grind my teeth. Although Fringe Girl had been my nickname in middle school for approximately three minutes (owing to my trademark bangs and my then-fave fringe suede jacket), Sondra continued to use it. Her way of reminding me that in the Brownstone social hierarchy, I clung to the fringe of popularity. Sondra liked Fringe Dwellers to know their place. Hers was queen of the Ruling Class. And Stanley was her newly anointed king.

Two minutes of conversation with her (them) was all I could stand. "What can I get you guys?" I asked.

Sondra smiled at me, and I was momentarily dazzled mute. Half-black, half-Japanese, she was truly an astonishing beauty. And she knew how her face affected mere mortals. Taking advantage of my temporary paralysis, she asked, "We haven't caught up yet. Tell me, Fringe, what's Liza Greene doing this summer? How *is* she?"

She asked like there was bound to be something

wrong. Sondra had always had it in for Liza. Maybe Liza's happy demeanor chafed Sondra the wrong way. Stanley, meanwhile, lowered his eyes at the mention of the girl he betrayed.

"She's *incredible*," I said. Sondra might've knocked Liza to her knees, but she hadn't punched Liza out cold. "She's in Bermuda with her parents, who are doing GREAT. She's living on the beach in an AMAZING house. It's the summer of her life. She's . . . she's hooked up with a professional golfer." Okay, that was stretching it a bit. Jerome's father was the club golf pro. But whatever.

Stanley said, "That's great, Dora. I'm glad she's well." He smiled sweetly, meaning it, probably relieved he hadn't caused permanent damage.

Sondra said, "Well, if she's having such a great summer in Bermuda, maybe she should consider staying down there all year."

"She is," I said, immediately regretting it, especially when I noticed Charlie, clearing dishes nearby, had overheard. He shot me a questioning look and mouthed, "Really?"

Shit. Liza had begged me not to tell Eli, and I'd done the next-best thing.

"I got a postcard from Noel," said Stanley, only too happy to steer the conversation away from Liza and onto the thorn in my side. Noel. The boyfriend who wasn't there.

"A postcard, cool," I said, as if I'd received hundreds from Noel. Inside, I was roiling with jealousy.

Stanley said, "Did you freak out?"

"Freak out?" I asked. "About what?"

"That he was chased by a bear!" said Stanley. Seeing my reaction, he said, "You didn't know?"

Obviously not! My jaw had dropped so far, it practically hit the table.

Stanley said, "Noel probably didn't want to tell you that story. Didn't want you to worry."

Oh, I was way, way beyond worried. Not about a frigging bear. But about *us*. "Look, I'm kind of busy," I said.

They gave me their breakfast order, and I took it to the kitchen.

In less than four minutes, Sondra and Stanley had destroyed my mood. I gave their orders to Ramon with hostility, slamming down the toaster button, spilling juice on the counter.

Stella started cutting a few bagels at the bread counter. "Eggs, bacon, toast. Again. I am so sick of the brunch menu. This place could be a real restaurant. It's a great location, for one thing. We could open it up to the general public, not just club members. Hire a castoff from *Top Chef* to cook. Put in a bar, and live music."

"Whatever," I said, not caring or sharing Stella's vision for what the Brick could be.

"What's wrong with you?" she asked.

"Nothing," I said.

"Bullshit," Stella replied. "Look what you did to that cinnamon bun."

I glanced down at the atomized crumbs of what had once been a sweet roll. I pointed through the cutout window between the kitchen and dining room. "See that girl out there? The unspeakably gorgeous one?"

"With the unspeakably sexy guy?"

"We're locked in a figurative cage match. Have been for about ten years now," I said.

"I recognize her," said Stella, peering through the window. "Sondra Fortune, right? She was in my squash class here, like, seven years ago."

"Was she an arrogant attention hog then, too?"

Stella said, "I barely paid attention to her."

That made sense. Stella was five years older and a lot cooler. If you asked me.

"Is that their order?" Stella pointed at my tray of OJ glasses and breadstuffs.

"Yup," I said. "If she doesn't leave a big tip, I'm going to . . ."

"To what?" asked Stella, grinning.

"I'm going to be very, very annoyed," I replied. "Don't think I won't!"

Stella laughed, and took my tray. "Let me serve them," she said. "Spare you the humiliation."

"Thanks," I said, not sure if fobbing them off on another waitress would make me less of a coward.

But Stella was already off, carrying the tray with one hand, rushing, a bit out of control. I watched through the cutout window as she stumbled against one customer, spun around, the tray jostling, nearly collided with Rosalyn in the aisle, and then dramatically twirled, tray tilting, its contents flying through the air, and landing precisely on target—Sondra Fortune's lap.

Stanley, meanwhile, not a drop of juice on him.

"Oh! My! God!" squealed Stella. "I am sosososo, sosososo SORRY! I'm a complete and utter *spaz*. There's no excuse for such clumsiness. I don't deserve to *live!*"

Sondra jumped up and batted away Stella's attempts to clean off her tennis skort with a napkin. Stanley stayed seated, blinking in confusion at the unexpected turn. As Sondra fumed and wiped at her orange splotches, she happened to look toward the kitchen and caught me watching through the window.

My instinct was to duck down. But instead, I smiled and waved. I had a weapon in my arsenal now. Stella was locked and loaded, a force to be reckoned with.

Sondra grumbled a bit. And then her well-crafted social grace kicked in. She smiled benignly at Stella.

"Accidents happen!" she sang, and sat back down in her chair. Stanley sighed with gratitude and relief.

Stella returned to the kitchen, and I applauded. "That was stupendous!" I raved to her. "You've got a gift! If there were a presidency for juice spillers, I'd run your election campaign!"

She poured another couple glasses of OJ. Her eyes were brimming with mischief. "Again?" she asked, holding up a glass.

I laughed, assuming she was kidding.

She said, "Unleash me, Dora."

She *was* serious. I stopped laughing, and felt a slight chill down my spine. Stella was a force to be reckoned with, I was sure of that. But I wondered if, one of these days, I'd be the one who had to reckon with her.

Rosalyn pushed between us. "Excuse me," she said. "While you two have your fun, some of us are trying to work."

Stella suggested going to Lester's after work, but I begged off. I really wanted to be alone on my first night of freedom. To treasure the privacy of the apartment. Test my solitude mettle. Besides, I was dead tired after a double shift, and I had to get up early to go to Friends tomorrow morning.

Planning my dinner menu of a pint of Heath Bar Crunch and a bag of microwave popcorn didn't take long. I chose my DVDs carefully: a double feature of *Team America: World Police* and *South Park: Bigger, Longer & Uncut*. I thought about opening one of Dad's bottles of wine, but that definitely didn't go with ice cream, so I stuck with Diet Coke.

I ate my junk and watched my junk. About halfway through the second movie, I realized I'd probably be doing pretty much the same thing even if my parents were home. Only, they'd be watching the movies and sharing the pint with me. If Noel were here, we'd be rolling on the couch, the ice cream left to melt on the table, the movie flickering away, unwatched.

The pang came. Not for my parents (although I conceded to appreciating them more in absentia). I missed Noel more that night than I ever had. I decided to sleep on the couch. The bed—where Noel and I had passed many divine afternoons—would be big, empty and lonely.

Turned out, the couch was short, lumpy and itchy. I slept decently anyway.

13

"And you are?" asked the plump blonde behind the front desk at Friends.

"Dora Benet," I announced myself. "You are Donna Snagg?"

She nodded. "You're the girl from last weekend. Dr. Gerritson said you'd be coming in."

"And here I am," I said.

"So I see," she replied.

Silence. Was I wrong to get the vibe that Donna Snagg didn't want me around? How could she not? The place was crawling with critters, dirty and smelly and noisy, poking through the cages in the front room. And those were just the people.

"Who are they all?" I asked, gesturing over to the couch and chairs, all jammed with women, men, kids.

"Prospective adopters," said Ms. Snagg. "Saturday is our busiest day of the week."

Last Saturday, the place had been deserted except for Zack and me. Brooklyn Heights really was a ghost town on summer holiday weekends. I noticed a couple kids my age puttering up and down the corridor, in and out of exam rooms. The volunteers who'd left Zack in the lurch last week? I should thank them for deserting him in his hour of great need. Got me this job.

"There you are," a voice called from the hallway. It was Zack, every inch as handsome as he was a week ago. "Donna, this is Dora Benet, the girl who saved my life last week. Thank God we found her. She showed more compassion and skill with the cats than anyone else in this place." Seeing the expression on Donna's face, he quickly added, "Including you."

I gasped. How mean! But Zack laughed when he saw her reaction.

Ms. Snagg said flatly, "It's wonderful you've found someone who meets your standards, Doctor."

Her feelings were hurt, and I made a mental note to try to be extra nice to her.

"I'm teasing you, Donna," he said, getting close enough to kiss her cheek. "You know this place would fall apart without you."

Ms. Snagg blushed furiously. A lot of women would be willing to take some gentle teasing from Zack in exchange for getting that close to him.

Zack issued his instructions. "We've got a full house today. Donna, you start interviewing these families and match them with pets. Ask Tim and Bob . . ."

". . . Tom and Rob," she corrected.

"Right. Tom and Rob should clean up out back, and take the dogs twice around the block. Dora will assist me in the exam rooms."

That sounded sexy. Didn't really know why, but my skin tingled a little.

Donna Snagg scowled at me. Make that super-duper nice.

"This way, Dora," said Zack.

I followed him down the tight hallway, feeling flattered as well as uneasy about being his special assistant. I wasn't sure I was qualified. Didn't I need a license?

"You were kind of harsh back there," I said.

"You mean to Donna?" he asked. "I can't help myself. She's always so serious. I just rib her a little, to relieve the pressure."

"What pressure?" I asked.

"Being a vet has its dark moments, Dora," he said.

We entered exam room one. Inside, a man in his forties, dressed in weekend-casual Dockers and a pink polo shirt, stood waiting. His pet, a fat cat, sat on the exam table and gave us a cynical (if optimistic) yawn.

"Good morning," said Zack.

"Morning," the man said. "This is Peaches."

Zack said, "Hello, Peaches," and rubbed the cat's neck. "And what brings you here?"

"She's fine," said the man, who didn't look too good himself. "She was my mother's cat for twelve years. A couple weeks ago, Mom had a fall. I had to move her to an assisted-living community. One that doesn't allow pets."

I watched Zack's face. He nodded grimly, like he'd been in this position before.

The man continued, "Friends has a reputation for never turning away animals for adoption."

"This is a twelve-year-old cat," said Zack, checking Peaches's teeth, feeling around her throat, peeking into her ears. "Her life expectancy isn't very long, and we have limited space."

"Please," said the man, starting to get upset. "I promised my mother I'd find a home for Peaches, and I've got nowhere else to turn."

I could see what Zack meant by veterinary work not being all purrs and tail wagging. This was damned uncomfortable to watch. Peaches herself seemed okay with it all. She looked at me and blinked lazily. I felt for her—losing her companion, not being wanted by anyone, feeling alone, yet still hopeful things would work out.

I said, "We'll take her," to the man.

Zack said, "We will?"

The man said, "Thank you! I really appreciate it. And, if possible, can you send me the contact information for the family that adopts Peaches?" He handed his business card to me. "My mom wants to make sure she's going to a good home."

I said, "Of course we will."

"Thanks again. You do God's work here. Bless you both," he said, then kissed Peaches on the forehead, and left the room.

Zack sighed again. Gustily. "Dora, you shouldn't've done that," he said.

"Why not? You do have that policy, right?"

"We do, but this cat is too old and sick to be adopted," he said. "I was going to recommend to"—Zack took the business card from me and read it—"Mr. Earnest O'Shey, that Peaches should be euthanized."

"Why? She looks great," I said, putting a protective hand on Peaches's back.

"Does she?" he asked. "Take a closer look."

I leaned down and scrutinized Peaches. She was a tabby with copper and black stripes, white socks, a white bib, and incredible orange eyes. "Okay, she's kind of fat, but that means she's well nourished," I said. "Her hair is shiny. Her nose is wet. Eyes bright. She's in peak health. She's old, but some cats live to be twenty, right? She's got years to go."

He pressed his stethoscope to her furry little chest.

"Most people want to adopt kittens. We've managed to place twelve-year-old cats before. It's possible. But Peaches has a serious problem. I couldn't, in good conscience, let her be adopted."

"Why not?" I asked. I rubbed the triangle of copper on Peaches's forehead. She leaned into my hand and purred.

Zack said, "Peaches is dying."

"*What?*"

He lifted up the cat's black lips and showed me her gums. "Do you see the tooth decay?"

Indeed, Peaches had gray and yellow teeth, jagged and spiky. The gums were white and mushy-looking. It was pretty gross. I nodded. He said, "That's symptom number one. Now feel around her throat."

"Lumpy," I said.

"Swollen lymph glands. Very swollen. That's symptom number two," he said. Zack turned away from Peaches to get a syringe in a drawer behind him. While he was doing that, I stroked Peaches on her back. She lifted her hind legs to get traction, and then purred like a pricey vacuum cleaner. Her whole little body vibrated under my hand, and she looked at me with orange eyes. They seemed to have tears in the corners.

"I'm going to take a sample of her blood to confirm my diagnosis," Zack said. "If I'm wrong and she doesn't have the disease, then Peaches will get a course of antibiotics and she'll probably be okay. I need you to hold her steady." Slowly, gently, Zack inserted the syringe into a spot on the cat's rear leg. She jerked, and I held her still.

"What disease are you looking for?" I asked. Peaches squirmed in my hands, and I felt awful that she had even a second of pain.

"Feline leukemia," he said. "It's a virus that attacks the immune system. Specific to cats only. Humans can't catch it. But it is highly contagious among cats. Considering Peaches's size and age, I'd say she hasn't had the virus long. When you see a cat with severe gingivitis and swollen glands, the immune system has broken down. It's a giveaway for fe-leuk."

The syringe was full of Peaches's blood now. Zack wiped the insertion spot with a swab, and prepared the sample for analysis. I soothed Peaches, who seemed to forget instantly that she'd just been poked with a needle. Back to purring contentedly, she kept rubbing her cheeks against my hand.

I'd pretty much fallen madly in love with her at this point.

Zack could be wrong about the feline leukemia. She might just have a sweet tooth and a bad cold.

He filled a test tube with her blood and then put two drops of liquid into it. "If she does have the virus, it's advanced. She has no immune system left. Antibiotics would fail, and her infections will kill her."

Zack shook the test tube. The blood inside turned black.

"Positive for antibodies," he said flatly.

We were both quiet for a minute. Peaches's purring was the only sound in the room. She had no idea she was sick and dying. She'd been taken away from her owner, dropped off in a strange place, pricked with needles, and still she purred against my fingers.

"You can't euthanize this cat," I said.

"I'm sorry, Dora," he said. "This is what I meant before. The hard part of the job."

"Is she in pain?"

"Apparently not!" he said, stroking her forehead. "Listen to her."

"And you think she has only a few days left?"

"A few days, a week," he guessed. "I don't think she'd like to spend it in a cage, in isolation. We can't expose the other cats to her."

I nodded, saw his point. "It's just a shame," I said. "To put a cat to sleep when she seems happy."

Zack said, "It is a shame. But at least we know that Peaches had a good life—which is more than I can say for our rescued street animals. And she'll have a peaceful death."

"What will happen to her body?"

"We use a crematory service in Park Slope. They do a daily pickup." He paused. "I think it'd be best if you asked Donna to come back here to help me."

"You don't think I can handle it?"

He raised his eyebrows. "Absolutely not. You're not ready for this. The first time I had to put an animal down, I was a wreck. Very embarrassing at veterinary school."

"How many times have you done it?" I asked, trying not to picture Zack as the Grim Reaper. Meanwhile, Peaches was sniffing around the exam table, contentedly exploring, leaning against my hip, her tail curling under my chin.

Zack said, "I haven't kept track. I'm a relatively young vet. In my two years at Friends, I've had to put down probably fifty animals."

I closed my eyes, picturing syringes with skulls and crossbones stenciled on the plunger. Then I pictured that needle parting Peaches's fur, penetrating her skin. The image made me gag a little. I'd finally felt a spark of love for an animal, and she was three minutes from death. I couldn't let that happen. I felt a sudden protectiveness, like a parent for a child.

He said, "Why don't you say good-bye to Peaches, and I'll go get Donna myself." Zack started toward the exam room door.

"Wait," I said, stopping him. "Let me just run an idea by you. These are the facts. Peaches is going to live for only a few more days. She's not in any apparent pain. If she's exposed to other cats, she might spread the virus, so she can't stay here. We both agree that she deserves a peaceful death, and that it's a shame she can't live out her life in a cozy home environment."

Zack said, "Correct."

"Let me take her home with me."

He looked shocked. "Why on earth would you want to do that?"

"I don't have any cats at home. I can give her a good last few days. My parents are out of town. Peaches can keep me company, and I'll return the favor." I tried to sound detached, holding back the most important factor in the equation, that I was already thinking of Peaches as my own pet and would sacrifice anything to prolong her life by any means necessary. Zack might think I was crazy, or at the very least emotionally starved and possibly unstable. And he might be right. What rational person invited a dying cat into her home?

If she really was dying. I looked at her, purring and sniffing and rubbing away, like she had all of her nine lives left. It was possible Zack was wrong, and that Peaches would pull through.

He studied my face. I might've let raw need flit across my brow. But I quickly shook it off and held firm.

"Give me the day to think about it," he said.

We got Peaches back into her carrier, and left her locked up in the exam room with a towel, food, water and a toy mouse. For the rest of the day, no cat could enter that room. Zack redirected me to menial tasks (I guess he didn't want me nagging him all day), doing comb outs, keeping excitable toddlers from rattling the cage doors in the front room, helping potential adoptive families fill out applications.

When I got the opportunity, I worked on Ms. Donna Snagg, complimenting her hair, smiling a lot, passing for sweet. I knew that if she backed me up, Zack would be more willing to let me take Peaches home. When Donna took a break for lunch, I womanned the front desk, answering the phone, making appointments. I filled out an adoption application for Peaches, just to dot i's, cross t's.

Throughout the day, I checked in on Peaches. And I checked out Zack. In terms of nonstop energy, he was off the charts. I had no idea what he was eating (or what he was on), but I wanted some. For an older guy, he had the zip and vim of an eight-year-old. I got exhausted just watching him. And, I had to admit, I couldn't help wondering what all that energy would be like in a more intimate situation. Zack, the tornado of love, gathering you up, tossing you around, sucking the air out of your lungs, and leaving you in a heap forty yards from where you started.

But as I constantly reminded myself, Zack was off-limits. He was way too old. He was my boss. And I was taken. For all I knew, Zack was married (no ring), or in a relationship (although he didn't mention any girlfriend, and didn't take a personal call from anyone all day).

At a slow minute in the late afternoon, it was just me and Donna at the front desk. Tim (Tom?) and Bob (Rob?) were in the kennels, and Zack was talking to an anxious dog owner in exam room three.

I said, "It's been great, being here. I doubt you remember, but you told me when I applied for the job that I'd probably never hear from you again."

"I don't remember," said Donna. "We had so many applicants."

Was she dismissive to everyone? "Dr. Gerritson works so hard! It must be rough on his family, to lose him on the weekends."

Donna said, "Dr. Gerritson lives alone, in a studio apartment not far from here. And if you're trying to ask me if he's single, the answer is: I don't know or care."

"Oh, you care," I said.

"I don't," she countered.

"Why not?" I asked. "Aren't you curious?"

She shook her head, but she was smiling a little. I thought I'd broken through her officious shell. She said, "It's not in my job description to meddle in the private lives of my colleagues. Just so you know. I don't gossip."

That was it. I gave up on her. She wasn't going

to like me, no matter how much syrup I poured on her.

Finally, closing time arrived. Tim/Tom and Bob/Rob—both Rising Juniors at St. Andrew's, Stella's old school—finished their tasks and left. Donna asked if she was needed about twenty times, and then she finally took a break. Zack and I were left alone to lock up. We made sure all the animals had enough food, water, litter for the night. I made a big show of giving Zack my official adoption application for Peaches. He read it, but didn't comment.

"You're stalling," I said.

"I think it's a lousy idea," he said. "Why do it to yourself?"

"Do what?"

"Get attached when you know it'll be temporary?" he said.

"You could say the same thing about a short-term relationship between people," I said. "There's intrinsic value to making an emotional connection, even if it's not meant to last."

He said, "Are you sure you're seventeen?"

The age of consent. "You think I'm wise for my years?"

Zack smiled. "I think you talk a good game, Dora."

"So I've convinced you?" I said. The more he resisted, the more I wanted him to give in. "I'm not a masochist, Zack. I just feel for Peaches. We looked each other in the eyeball. Through the eyeball, if you know what I mean."

On cue, Peaches meowed loudly.

"I see something special in her," I said.

"I see something special in you," he said.

Zack looked down at me (did I mention that he was tall?), and seemed to be wrestling with a decision. If I didn't know better, I'd say that he was trying to decide whether he should kiss me.

He appeared to have made up his mind. "Okay, I accept your application. You can take Peaches home."

"Yea!" I said.

"Here's how it's going to work," he said. "I'm going to give you some medicine for her. She should take one pill every morning. I want a progress report from you every day by phone. If she starts to look bad—if she can't walk or is unresponsive—call me and I'll come get her right away."

"Done," I said.

"Can you lift her?" he asked, sliding her carrier out from under the counter. I bent down and picked it up by the handle. It was heavy and bulky. He handed me another bag full of food, a plastic litter box and some clumping litter.

Like I said before, I was weak like meerkat. My arm muscles strained after five seconds of holding Peaches. "Okay, I can do this," I said.

"Maybe I should walk you and Peaches home," said Zack, taking the carrier and litter bag out of my hands. Our fingers brushed during the transfer. My breath caught.

"We go?" asked Zack, already headed down the hallway.

"Right behind you," I said.

"I think she likes it here," said Zack.

We let Peaches out of the carrier in my dining room. She started sniffing the air, rubbing her cheeks against the table legs, the chairs, the walls. Marking her territory.

Zack showed me how to wrap the pain pill in a piece of turkey, and we gave Peaches a dose. She licked her chops and then her paws.

"The pill might make her sleepy," he said. "We should set up the litter before she takes a nap." We put the box in the powder room on the first floor of our duplex, and then showed Peaches where it was. We also showed her the food and water bowls in the kitchen.

"That's it," said Zack. "Aren't cats easy?"

Once that business was concluded, I remembered that Zack, having carried fifteen pounds of cat and fourteen pounds of litter for six blocks in ninety-five-degree heat, might need a drink.

He confirmed this by saying, "Hot in here."

My parents had a philosophical opposition to air-conditioning. I wasn't sure what was their objection to cool air. They rambled about energy consumption and the environment, the unhealthy shift from outdoor to indoor temperatures, the efficiency of oscillating fans. I think they were just too lazy to haul big units up the three flights of stairs to our apartment.

I said, "Diet Coke?"

"That'd be great," he said.

Feeling the heat myself, I got a bright idea. I gave Zack a can of soda and then ran upstairs to the top floor of our duplex. I found a pair of my dad's swim shorts in his dresser. They were long and baggy, an easy fit for Zack. I went in my room and snagged one of my bikinis, a beach tote and a couple bath towels.

Coming back downstairs, I saw that Peaches had already found a nice spot to sleep on one of our living room couches. "She looks cozy," I said.

"All this excitement," he said. "She'll probably sleep for a while."

"Have you been to the floating pool barge yet?" I asked.

"The what?"

I told him about the pool, the evening hours. If we ran, we might catch the last swim of the day, from 8:30 to 10:00. The twilight swim. I'd yet to barge under the stars, and was just dying to.

And it'd be very romantic.

Zack said, "Sounds fun. But I don't have a . . ."

I held up Dad's red suit. Zack took it, held it against his hips and said, "Do you have it in black?"

We speed walked down Joralemon Street to the pool barge. The guy handing out wristbands said we got the last two spots. We changed in the appropriate-gendered locker rooms, and met on the patio. Sure enough, the pool was as crowded as on a weekday morning. I half expected to find Stella lounging around, but it was a Saturday night. She was probably at a bar or club, fending off hundreds of admirerers.

Zack said, "This is incredible! You can see the whole skyline."

The view was incredible. The Brooklyn and Manhattan Bridges, the ribbons of red and white headlights of cars on the BQE and the FDR Drive, the silver pointed towers of the Empire State and Chrysler Buildings. The sun was just setting behind the Statue of Liberty. The air had cooled to the high eighties. It'd be dark soon.

The view of Zack in trunks: Also incredible. His legs were long and well muscled. A bit hairy, but that was okay. His chest, lean and tight, had hardly any hair, which I liked. The belly? Not exactly a six-pack, but flat enough to eat off of.

I watched his eyes to see if he was going to check me out. Not that I had a lot to examine. Sadly, Zack seemed more captivated by the river view than me. Which was probably a good thing.

He said, "Shall we?" and jumped in. I followed. Zack started swimming in circles around me. Then he dove under, and surprised me by swimming between my legs (!!!!). I watched him glide through water, green lit by submerged fixtures, wavy and sleek. When he sputtered to the surface, he said, "I can do five somersaults in a row."

And he did. My record was three, and I got water up my nose, which made me sneeze ("Hey, you, in the green!"). We tried to outdo each other at handstands and breath holding, too. He won all our contests. I didn't mind. He was just so damn *happy* to be playing, and winning. I started to wonder if Zack spent all his time with four-legged mammals, and not nearly enough with the two-legged variety. In the city, even hot docs could get lonely.

The lifeguard blew the whistle at 10:00 on the dot. Zack said, "No way!" like a six-year-old, and actually slapped the water. It was cute, his display.

I felt glad to have showed Zack a good time. It was my way of thanking him for letting me take Peaches. And, full disclosure, I really wanted to hang out, just for a while, with a man. Especially a sexy one like Zack. I missed Noel for his essential Noel-ness. But I also missed the attention of a man.

Zack and I changed back into our clothes, and

met up on the gangplank that connected the pool to the "beach." We started to walk back up Joralemon Street toward Garden Place. Zack got quiet.

I said, "Girlfriend waiting at home?"

He laughed. "No girlfriend."

We reached my block. "Do you want to come up, check on Peaches?"

I meant it as a friendly invitation. I wasn't trying to seduce him, or act like a teenage succubus, luring innocent men to their doom. But Zack looked at me like I'd offered to perform a sex act right there on the street.

"I'm sure Peaches is fine," he said.

"Okay, Doc," I said, both disappointed and relieved. "I'll beep you if she seems weird. And I wasn't, you know, by inviting you up. I wasn't . . . I have a boyfriend."

"I bet you do," he said. He reached for my hand, and put my dad's wrung-out bathing suit into it.

14

"I am crushing," I told Stella the next morning at the Brick. "Moderate to high level of intensity."

"The hot vet?" she asked, chewing on a bagel.

"How'd you know?"

"It had to be either the vet, or Ramon," she said.

Ramon, hearing his name, said, *"Qué?"*

Rosalyn, nearby, folding napkins, said, "You've got two jobs, you're studying for the SATs and you've got time for a crush?"

"You don't schedule a crush," I said. "A crush squeezes itself in." Meanwhile, I hadn't spent ten minutes on SAT prep.

"Don't listen to Roz," said Stella. "You know what all work and no fun makes *her.*"

Rosalyn put her hands on her hips, rotated her head around on her neck Latina style and said, "You don't have any idea what I do for fun, Stella. And it's a good thing, 'cause my idea of fun would blow your freaking head off. You'd lose your *mind*, just talking about how I have fun."

"Less taunting, more chopping," said Jorge, fretting, checking his watch, as usual.

Whispering, I asked Rosalyn, "Would it blow my head off, your idea of fun?"

"Trust me, you can't handle the fun," said Rosalyn.

Stella laughed. Surprisingly, Rosalyn joined in. I'd yet to see them laugh together. The sight inspired me.

"So, listen, guys," I said. "You know my parents are out of town. Let's have a girls' night in tonight. A sleepover, even. Pizza, ice cream, we can shave our legs and talk about boys. You could meet Peaches, who is the most adorable kitty ever."

Stella blinked and said, "You're delivery is so deadpan, Dora. I'm never sure if you're kidding."

"She was kidding about shaving our legs. The rest of it was real," said Rosalyn—correctly.

"Damn," said Stella. "I've always wanted to do a group shave."

"So we're on?" I asked.

"I like it," said Jorge, butting in. "Then you can get each other over here early tomorrow morning."

"And why would we do that?" asked Stella.

Jorge said, "Mr. Rupert Sandstone is flying to New York from his home base in Miami this week, and he plans on spending part of his stay here at the Brick."

"Who?" I asked.

"Rupert Sandstone. He owns the Brick. The building itself, the club—and the restaurant," said Jorge. "You didn't notice that your paychecks are is-sued by Sandstone Inc.?"

"Not really," I said.

Stella said, "Will we get to meet him?" She seemed intrigued by the idea of getting up close and personal with the honcho.

"You, Stella, might even get to serve him," said Jorge. "But we've got a lot of extra work to do, clean-ing this place until it shines. If Mr. Sandstone isn't happy, he could fire us all." A fresh drizzle of nervous sweat leaked out of his forehead, which he mopped up with a napkin.

Charlie, just coming into the kitchen from the dining room, had to be brought up to speed about the upcoming inspection. "He might decide to give us all raises, too," said Charlie.

Jorge said, "You think the rich stay rich by giving money away?" and then went to fret elsewhere.

Charlie buttered a raw English muffin, took a bite and said to me, "I think I might've done a bad thing."

"Don't you want to toast that?" I asked.

"I told Eli in an e-mail that you said Liza might

be staying in Bermuda," he said. "She got really upset, and started firing off e-mails to Liza, who denied everything. Liza sent an e-mail to me to tell you you're in deep shit with her."

"Why didn't she tell me herself?" I asked.

"Liza said she's too angry to e-mail you," he said. "Eli's kind of mad at you, too."

"Even when we're in different countries, I manage to piss them off," I said.

"I have guilt," he said. Charlie was very cute when he was guilty, with his sideburns and cheekbones and pursed lips. I bet Eli couldn't stay mad at him for a second.

"Forget it," I told him. "Leave the guilt to us Jews—we're programmed to handle it. I'll straighten things out with Eli and Liza." Didn't know how. But I was sure to get some bright idea. They always came along, often striking when I least expected them.

"I want you to know," he said. "I'm a little mad at you, too."

"Why?" I asked. If anything, I should be annoyed with him for telling Eli about Liza possibly staying in Bermuda.

He smiled and said, "You didn't invite me to your leg-shaving party."

I laughed. "I'll let you feel my stubble tomorrow, okay?"

"Deal," he said.

❅   ❅   ❅

"So this is your apartment," said Rosalyn, as I led her into our duplex. She was panting slightly from the hike up the stairs. I cursed the climb every day, but my legs were stronger for it. "Nice," she said.

Stella had gone to her place in the North Heights to pack a bag. Rosalyn would borrow what she needed from me. I was a bit worried that my clothes wouldn't fit her. She had a caboose. I'd just give her gym shorts and an oversized T-shirt.

"Wanna see my room?" I offered. "This way."

She followed me upstairs and I ta-da'ed when I opened the door to my lair.

"It's small, but it's mine," I said, bouncing on the bed, kicking off my sneaks.

Rosalyn said, "I like the purple walls and the shag carpet. And this isn't small. It's big, compared to my room—and I share it with my two younger sisters."

"I feel a Monty Python skit coming on. 'I had to walk to school ten miles every day.' 'That's nothing. I had to walk ten miles, without shoes.' 'Luxury! I had to walk ten miles—without *feet*.'"

Rosalyn laughed ruefully. "I'm not complaining, Dora," she said. "You just can't understand where I'm coming from. Literally. Have you ever been to the Bronx?"

"I've been to Yankee Stadium plenty of times," I said.

"You and Stella think I'm this school-obsessed workaholic. You'd be the same way if you didn't have rich parents to fall back on. I'm all I've got. My ticket to an apartment like this in a neighborhood like this, is by doing what I do." Rosalyn tapped her temple. "I'm focused, Dora."

Peaches jumped onto my bed. She'd already picked a favorite spot for herself on the sweater shelf in my closet, which was not easy to get to. She had to leap about four feet onto the shelf, a show of power and agility that befit a healthy cat. It'd been two days, and Peaches seemed happier and livelier as each hour passed. I was convinced that Zack got her diagnosis wrong. That my care and love had cured her.

"Here she is," I said. Speaking in an annoying baby voice, I cooed to my cat, "Hello, Peaches. This is Rosalyn. She comes from the Bronx, *yes, she does*. And she doesn't have rich parents, *no, she doesn't*."

"Man, I must really like you," said Rosalyn. "Anyone else ribbed me like that, I'd give them the treatment."

"The treatment?"

"Yell at them in Spanish at a hundred miles an hour, a lot of finger wagging in the face, shoulder shaking, tongue clicking."

"I'd love to see that, actually," I said.

"Shut up and move over."

She sat on the bed with Peaches between us. We

gave that cat the full-body massage of her life, a four-handed rubdown. Peaches purred so loudly, I felt the vibrations in my feet.

"All's I'm saying," I started, "is that if you died tomorrow, you wouldn't go to heaven wishing you'd put in an extra shift at the Brick."

"See, that's a perfect example of how you don't get it," she said. "My mother had me when she was seventeen. Your age. Me? I'm focused on my future. I'd die happy, knowing I had a plan to lift myself up. My life would be meaningless if I chased after guys like Stella, or if I frittered away my potential like you."

"Hey," I said. "I don't fritter."

"Why the hell are you waitressing?" she asked. "You should have some rich-kid internship in the city, or some save-the-world volunteer job."

"For your information," I said, "I gave up the chance to save the world this summer so I could slice bread at the Brick. There are a lot of hungry tennis players who desperately need toast, and I give it to them."

Rosalyn laughed. She was laughing a lot tonight. While stroking Peaches (in Cat Heaven-on-Earth at the moment), she said, "Maybe you're just too young to take yourself seriously."

"I'm only three years younger than you," I said.

"I'm not talking about years," said Rosalyn. "I'm talking about your soul."

BUZZ. The door. Had to be Stella. Rosalyn visibly tensed at the sound of her arrival. Perhaps Rosalyn knew that Stella would not want to discuss the age of her soul. Or how possessing an aged soul—an aged *anything*—was a good thing.

I still believed that Rosalyn and Stella, opposites on the surface, would find a depth of common ground if they dug for it. I saw myself as the go-between, the one who might make it possible for Stella to loosen up Roz, and for Roz to, er, tighten up Stella. Or maybe I was delusional. Only one way to find out.

I buzzed Stella in. She trudged up the stairs. When she crossed the threshold of our apartment, she handed me a brown paper bag, cold to the touch.

"Six-pack," she said.

"Diet Coke?" I asked hopefully.

"Brooklyn Lager," she said. "And a pack of Marlboro Lights in there, too."

Cigarettes now? "You don't smoke," I reminded Stella.

"Sometimes I do," she said.

"Outside," I insisted.

"Afraid your parents will smell five-day-old cigarette smoke when they come back?"

I shook my head. "No. I'll be disgusted by the smell, and puke on the furniture. And the smell of puke lingers. Longer than cigarettes."

Rosalyn said, "Can we turn on the air?"

"No air," I said.

"No air?" they asked in unison.

"My parents don't believe in air-conditioning," I said.

Stella ranted, "They don't believe in it? Is air-conditioning like Santa Claus? The Easter Bunny?"

"Even in the Bronx, we have air-conditioning," said Roz.

They laughed at my expense. I was fine with it, as long as they mocked me together.

"Incoming," I said, tapping my noggin. "Brilliant ideas. They strike when you least expect it."

"Waiting," said Stella, cracking open a beer.

"We have a plastic blow-up wading pool for the deck," I said. "I'll fill it with the hose, and we can sit in it. Instant relief from the heat."

"Will we all fit?" asked Roz.

"Definitely," I said. "It's eight feet across, two feet high. Like an oversized bathtub." I brought them through the living room and showed them our apartment's deck. It was built on the roof of our downstairs neighbor's extension. Three stories above the ground, the deck, our prized 450 square feet of outdoor space, overlooked the courtyards on Garden Place and Henry Street. My dad had planted two dozen pots with flowering plants, mainly geraniums, marigolds and petunias. They looked a little droopy, and I remembered

I was supposed to water them daily. Oops. We had a Weber grill, and a teak table and chair set out. Three interlocking strings of multicolored Christmas bulbs were twined along the deck railing.

Stella said, "Whew. Much better outside."

Roz agreed. "This is a great deck. Private, too." A huge maple tree blocked the view from Henry Street. We were higher than most of the other decks on Garden Place.

"It's bikini safe," I said. Our neighbors to the right could see us from their windows, but all the lights were out next door.

"What's the point of wearing a bikini if no one sees it?" asked Stella. A light in her eye went on. "Hey, I bet we could go naked up here."

Rosalyn said, "Let's not and say we did."

Stella and Roz went back inside and up to my room to look for bathing suits. I found the deflated pool in the deck shed, crumpled in a big plastic ball. I put my lips to the nozzle and started blowing. I nearly died. My lungs hadn't had such a workout since the last time I jogged—a year ago, to impress a boy (didn't).

Once the pool was inflated, I turned on the deck hose. The water was pretty cold. Like ice actually, but it'd warm up (I hoped). I gave the plants a drink, and then left the hose in the pool to fill. I went back inside.

I found Stella and Roz, wearing my bathing suits, standing in the kitchen with the fridge door open.

"There's enough food in here to feed a family of six for a week," said Roz, poking around on the fully stocked shelves.

I blushed. "My parents. They go overboard with the FreshDirect. And my dad thinks he's a chef."

"Your dad cooks? I can't remember the last time I had a home-cooked meal," said Stella. "Anorexic mother. Workaholic father. If I want dinner, I have to order it or open a can of something, cross my fingers and hope I don't die of botulism."

Roz said, "My mom brings home a cartload of groceries, and it's gone inside twenty-four hours."

"But at least she cooks for you," said Stella.

"She works nights at the hospital," said Roz. "She's an RN. I do most of the cooking for me and my sisters, which means a lot of beans and rice."

"Dad in the picture?" asked Stella, removing a container of tuna salad, a tomato and a loaf of bread.

"Nope," said Roz, choosing for herself some sliced turkey breast, a brick of cheddar and the coleslaw Dad made with farmer's market cabbage.

"How many sisters?" asked Stella of Roz.

"Two at home," she said. "Another one moved down the block with her boyfriend."

"I've got a sister, too," I threw in. "She's at sleep-away camp."

Roz smiled at me in a "that's nice, dear" way. Then she asked Stella, "You're an only child, right?"

"Why do you say that?" asked Stella.

I'd assumed the same thing. She never mentioned a sibling. I said, "You're not?"

"I had a brother," said Stella. "Older. He died of brain cancer when I was five. He's still a big presence in our house." She made a spooky face.

"Like a ghost?" I asked.

Stella said, "More like, when my brother died, my parents turned into ghosts."

That killed the banter. Stella: Not as born-lucky as I'd thought. I could tell Rosalyn's opinion of Stella had softened.

"I've done some stuff with psychics, tried to contact Henry," said Stella. "But I never believed anything they said. Henry was seven when he died. I just assumed his spirit would stay the same age. What seven-year-old is going to cross the astral plane to tell me that I needed to travel more often? One psychic said Henry thought I should redecorate my bedroom because my curtains were depressing me."

"Were they?" I asked.

"What seven-year-old knows from curtains?" asked Stella. "Or depression?"

"Maybe when you die, your soul becomes an interior decorator," I said.

"I can see the show now on TLC," said Stella. *"Design from Beyond."*

While they finished making sandwiches, I ran upstairs and changed and then checked the pool. It was full of freezing water. The night air, though, was thick as gravy and just as hot.

Stella and Roz brought their food outside. We sat at the table in our suits and ate. At seven o'clock, it was still sunny and bright. The heat sure did make beer taste good. But I decided one would be my limit. Roz had one, too. Stella was into her second. When she finished eating, she lit a cigarette.

Roz put a big toe in the water. "Yow," she said. But she put her whole foot in, and the other.

I stood next to her, in water halfway up the shin. Stella came in, too. We talked about the Brick. About nothing. We eased into sitting positions. The water was slowly heating up, thanks to our body temperature. Eventually, we were able to stretch out our legs and lean back against the sides of the pool.

"That's better," I said.

"Let me have one of those smokes," said Rosalyn.

Stella got her one, and the two of them lay in the pool, smoking and drinking, talking idly about Daniel Craig. They were totally relaxed, happy, comfortable.

And it was all because of me.

I was the hostest with the mostest.

Peaches wandered outside, sniffed in our direction and then lay down on the deck, not a care in the world, much less a fatal disease. I got a warm feeling in my belly. A flash of the future, or what my life could be. What my life actually was. These two women liked me, were hanging out with me, not treating me like a kid at all. I was an equal, an adult who could fend for herself, just as they did.

"This is the life," I said.

Stella smiled and took a swig of her beer. "This is," she agreed.

Roz slid forward, her head sinking under the water for a second. When she emerged, she squeezed out her hair and asked, "So, Dora, what do you have in that fully stocked fridge for dessert?"

I could take a hint. I volunteered to serve up some ice cream. While dishing Ben & Jerry's into bowls, I realized I hadn't thought about Noel in hours.

Zack's face rose suddenly in my consciousness. I imagined him here, just the two of us in the wading pool, our skin slippery, the water beading on our chests. . . .

"Hey, Dora!" called Stella. "Don't let the ice cream melt!"

15

July 27, 2008
To: abenet@brownstone.edu
From: lgreene@brownstone.edu
Re: Stanley Nable

I think I've figured out what happened. Stanley and Sondra came to the Brick. They asked about me. You painted a rosy picture of my life in South Hampton to make them seethe with jealousy. Charlie overheard, and he told Eli that I wasn't coming back to Brooklyn. She sent an angry e-mail to me. I got mad at you and your big flapping gums.

You'll be happy to know that I've forgiven you (yet again). The truth is, me and Jerome broke up. I'm over him. He's sexy and romantic—and here, which I realized was what I liked most about him. How many relationships have been forged out of mere proximity? The whole boy-next-door thing. Anyway, I've thus far received FOUR pleading e-mails from Stanley begging me to return to Brownstone. He wants me back, Dora! Can you believe? Know what? I'm leaning.

July 28, 2008
To: lgreene@brownstone.edu
From: abenet@brownstone.edu
Re: you, going crazy

Has your brain melted in all that sun? You were so DONE with Stanley last spring. He's with Sondra Fortune now. I saw them very much together. He probably only wants you because I told him you're in love with someone else! Not that you're not highly desirable, and any man alive would be grateful for three seconds of your attention. But do you really want to get back together with Stanley? You've broken up twice already, and the last time was a total train wreck. He's probably sick of Sondra's queenly demands. And who wouldn't be?

July 29, 2008
To: abenet@brownstone.edu
From: estomp@brownstone.edu
Re: Wurst

If I eat one more piece of sausage, you'll hear me scream in Brooklyn. Much as it horrifies me—in theory—I've come to realize something important about myself: I'm a homebody. You know how I hate to admit to any weakness (hate to even type the word "weakness"). I'm so homesick, I'm giving you and Liza both a free pass on that whole "Don't tell Eli" situation. I'm counting the days—eighteen—until I fly back to New York. And once I'm on home turf, I'm never leaving the city again. I mean it. Harvard is no longer an option. It's Columbia or NYU or nowhere. Since I'm never leaving home again, I should consider myself lucky that my home happens to be the greatest city in the world.

July 30, 2008
To: estomp@brownstone.edu
From: abenet@brownstone.edu
Re: Rain

Right now, in the city you miss so freaking much, it's ninety degrees, raining, thundering, lightning. I'm in my room, alone with Peaches (my cat. You heard me; I adopted her. What my parents don't know—yet—can't hurt me), watching the light show in the window, and hoping my parents aren't driving through this weather, wherever they are right now—I think New Hampshire.

Peaches is purring on my lap as I type. She's the warmest, cuddliest, cutest, sweetest ball of fluff in the world. I love her as much as I could love my own human baby. It's like I'm a teenage mother. Zack (hot

vet) called tonight, to check in about Peaches. In my
aloneness, in the storm, I asked him if he wanted to
come over. For the three seconds between my offer
and his saying "It's really late," I saw the whole scene
of how it might play out if he said, "On my way." I
guess I'm glad he's not coming. It'd be over between
me and Noel if he did. What does it say that after six
weeks apart, I'm attracted to another guy?

"Yup, you've come to the right place! It's Noel's voice
mail! And you should really leave a message, as soon
as you hear the . . . *BEEEEP*!"

[SOUND OF A HEAVY, WET, DESPERATE AND FRUSTRATED SIGH,
AND THEN AN AGGRESSIVE CLICK OF PUSHING THE END BUTTON
AS HARD AS POSSIBLE.]

[POSTCARD OF A LOON ON A LAKE. ON THE FLIP SIDE, A BARELY
LEGIBLE HANDWRITTEN NOTE.]

Dora! We're in Pittsfield, Maine, in a cabin on
a lake. We have seen many loons. Your father went fishing and caught a perch! Joya
is very happy at camp, as I'm sure you're glad
to hear. The Volvo has not fallen apart. We
hope you're enjoying your taste of independence, which will come to a crashing halt
when we get home. Love, Mom and Dad

16

"How old do you think he is?" I asked Stella. We were looking through the cutout window between the kitchen and dining room at the Brick at Rupert Sandstone. We'd spent the last few days busting our humps, cleaning and polishing, in anticipation of his arrival. And now he, and an entourage of three assistants, was here in the dining room. Jorge rushed out to greet him. For all our toil, Sandstone didn't seem inclined to tour the kitchen. He sat down at a table with Jorge. His assistants, all men, sat at the next table over.

"Hard to guess age," said Stella. "Fifty-five? Sixty? Who cares how old he is when he's that good-looking."

"He's older than my dad," I said.

"So? A man can't be handsome if he's mature?" she replied. "Besides, you can subtract five years of age for every million he's worth. Which would make Rupert Sandstone about five years old." Stella paused, mused. "I've always wanted to date a younger man."

I was appalled. Was she serious? Even more

shocking, Rosalyn laughed. "What are you waiting for?" asked Roz. "Go see if he needs a drink."

"I will," said Stella.

Roz and I watched Stella sail through the door into the dining room. Her ponytail (and ass) swishing from side to side, she sidled up to Sandstone, smiled and asked him a question. He responded, of course, since he was male and this was Stella. He grinned back at her like the lion who ate the okapi, touched her aproned hip (!), and gave her his order. She leaned into his hand (!!), smiled brightly, which nearly blinded me from thirty feet away, and started swishing back to the kitchen.

Rosalyn said, "Shameless."

I had to agree. Not to be judgey—I was firmly in the camp of people doing their own thing—but the display was gross. Stella was brazenly flirting with a much older man who happened to be her boss's boss. It made me feel unclean on her behalf.

Jorge, I noticed, had observed Stella's behavior with the same uncomfortable disapproval. He frowned, and it made his mustache droop.

Charlie came up behind Rosalyn and me and looked into the dining room. He said, "Sandstone is at my table? I'd best get out there."

"Stella beat you to it," I said.

"She can have him. I'm sneaking out," he said, removing his apron and throwing it in the hamper.

And then he split like a banana. I'd never seen him move so fast. You'd think he had a date or something. It was closing time. Only a few straggler customers remained, and they were gearing up to leave.

Rosalyn said, "I'm going to take off, too."

"Wanna come over?" I asked. Being alone during the storm the other night was harder than I'd expected. If it weren't for Peaches, I might've freaked out a little. No rain predicted for tonight, but company would be nice.

"How long until your parents come back?" she asked.

"Three days," I said.

"You'll survive," she said, and threw her apron in the hamper. She called a good-bye to her cousins at the grill and walked out.

No reason I should stick around. Unless Stella wanted to go to Lester's. Maybe Nick was working, and he'd serve up a few wine spritzers, just the way I liked 'em: heavy on the spritz.

Right on cue, Stella came rushing into the kitchen. "Mr. Sandstone wants a steak and fries. Rare."

Ramon groaned. He'd just finished cleaning the grill.

Stella took one look at his face. "I'll do it," she said. "You go."

Ramon bowed and gave her the *muchas gracias* treatment.

"You can cook?" I asked.

"I can grill a steak," she said. "I can fry a potato, too."

"I thought we might check out Lester's. Play the free-drink game."

"What game?" asked Stella, taking a sirloin fillet out of the fridge and firing up the grill.

"How you order a drink and then a guy offers to buy you another before you finish," I said.

"Oh, that," said Stella. "I'm not really in a Lester's kind of mood tonight. But you go. Nick should be there. He'll take care of you."

Take care of me? What, was I an infant in need of supervision? Was I incapable of taking care of myself? I'd been surviving just fine on my own for the better part of a week. Except for a few shaky moments (during a thunderstorm; totally understandable), I'd been solid as granite from the state of New Hampshire, which was where my parents were presently, 350 miles away.

"I get it," I said snidely.

"What do you get?" Stella asked.

"Nothing," I said.

Stella flipped the steak. "Mr. Sandstone owns a few other properties, too," she said. "He's got a nightclub in Miami, in South Beach."

"You've been Googling?" I asked.

She nodded. "I like to be prepared."

The steak smelled wonderful, except I'd lost my appetite. "The club in Miami," I said. "Live music?"

"That's right, Dora," said Stella, plating the meat. She checked her reflection in the chrome over the food lamps. "Oh, no. This will NOT do." Stella pulled out her ponytail, and flung her head around. Her hair bounced obediently. She checked her teeth for lipstick, and then practiced a seductive smile.

I wondered just how far she'd go. Then again, I wasn't sure I wanted to know. What a prig I am, I thought. Why was I so bothered by the idea of Stella using her sex appeal for professional purposes on a rich, much (much) older man? Was that so wrong?

Yuck. It totally was.

"He might be married," I said.

Stella said, "Your point?"

"I'm going home," I said.

"See you tomorrow," she said, picking up the plate and taking it back out to the now-empty (except for Sandstone, Jorge and three unfed assistants) dining room.

Nine o'clock on a Thursday night, with absolutely nothing to do and no one to do it with. I couldn't sit at home again, no matter how adorable Peaches was.

I went to the movies. I picked a PG-13 romantic comedy starring Anna Faris. I got my 'corn and entered the theater. Sitting in the best seat in the house, right in the middle of the front row mezz, I spotted the one person I least wanted to see me alone like a loser at the movies.

Her eagle eye—nothing embarrassing went by her—caught me. She waved. Escape was impossible. Groaning, I walked toward her.

"Fringe! What a . . . pleasant surprise," said Sondra Fortune.

No way she'd be here alone, too, I thought. Stanley had to be nearby—he of the "come back to me" e-mails to Liza—or else one of the ass kissers she called friends.

"I'll assume you've sent your 'friends' to buy you popcorn," I said, leaning on the railing in front of her.

"I don't eat theater popcorn. It's like five thousand calories a cup. Or maybe you don't know that," she said, glancing at the box in my hands.

"Okay, I'll be leaving now. . . ."

"Oh, Dora, just shut up and have a seat," said Sondra, patting the empty chair next to her. "You are alone, aren't you?"

"Maybe," I replied lamely.

She laughed. "Since you're alone, and I am also by myself, I don't see why two former frenemies can't sit in relative proximity and watch the show, without speaking or enjoying each other's company outright."

"I don't suppose I can refuse after you asked so nicely," I said, ducking under the railing and sitting next to Sondra. "We won't speak of this."

"Of course not," she said.

Sondra and I smiled at each other, and I couldn't help feeling a little warmth in the heart region. For all our sworn hatred, we understood each other in a way that rivaled my friendships with Eli and Liza. Couldn't explain it. I guess Sondra brought out the otherwise repressed bitchy side of my personality. It was a relief to let her out once in a while.

We watched the comedy. It had a few moments. I'd give it a B+. Sitting with Sondra? Around the same grade. We laughed at the same jokes. The cruder ones. When we walked outside, we lingered for a few minutes under the marquee. Neither of us was in a hurry to leave.

"Where's Stanley tonight?" I asked.

"Are we going to stand here on the street?" she asked. "Or are we doing something?"

Obviously, Sondra was desperate for companionship, if she was asking to hang with me. And who was I to deny her? I wasn't a mean person. Just cynical. And I was just as desperate as she was.

"This way," I said.

As we walked, I sensed her hesitation. Also, a little gratitude. Even the Queen of the Ruling Class got a little lonely in the long summer months.

"Stanley and I," she said, "broke up."

That explained his e-mails to Liza. Talk about re-bound. "Lost interest?" I asked.

She nodded. "As soon as I had him."

"But you managed to stick it out for, what, three whole months? That's practically marriage track for you."

"Don't I know it!" she said. "I would have ended it sooner if either of us went out of town for the summer. I was stuck here, and so was he."

Stuck? With her fabulous internship at *Project Runway*? "How's the job?"

"It's degrading," she said. "I barely get to see the stars of the show. I spend three hours a day answering the phone and going on latte runs." Sondra caught my expression. "Are you so surprised that an internship sucks?"

"I'm surprised you're admitting it," I said.

"I'm kind of surprised, too," she said.

"Wanna meet my new cat?" I asked. We were rounding the corner of Garden Place. My apartment was on the way home for Sondra anyway.

"Is it dewormed?" she asked. "And deloused?"

"Yes or no."

"Why not?"

I unlocked my building's front door, and told her the story of Peaches. We entered my apartment, and Peaches rushed to greet us, purring and sidling between our legs, rubbing her cheeks against our ankles.

One look and Sondra said, "This is not a sick cat."

"Vets can't be right all the time," I said.

"Does Noel know about Zack, the hot vet?"

"Zack is way too old for me," I said. "It's outside the realm of fantasy." Well, not exactly. "And Noel knows that I'm devoted to him."

"In other words, Noel hasn't heard one word about him."

"Not even a syllable," I said. He hadn't heard a syllable about anything, but I didn't tell her that.

I showed her into the living room, which, despite knowing me for a decade, she'd never seen before. She wasn't, apparently, wowed. She said, "Red walls. Interesting," and then got comfortable on the couch. I fetched Diet Cokes and served hers in a glass.

"Your new pal, Stella Walters," said Sondra after taking a sip. Peaches jumped up next to her on the couch.

"What about her?" I asked.

"Watch your back," said Sondra.

"Is she behind me with a knife?" I asked.

Stroking Peaches's head, Sondra said, "According to my sources at St. Andrew's, Stella Walters was the kind of popular we don't have at Brownstone."

I was still a bit fuzzy on the nuances of popularity

at my own school, let alone St. Andrew's. "We have parties at Brownstone," I said. Notably, Sondra took me to a Ruling Class "earring party," where the girls put one of their earrings in a bowl. The boys took turns reaching into the bowl, and won the prize of getting to suck on the ear from whence it came for the remainder of the night. Goes without saying, I declined to drop my hoop into the bowl.

"Brownstone parties are PG-13 compared to St. Andrew's," she said. "You know this."

I did. Stella's school had a druggie reputation. But Stella wasn't a druggie. She was an alchy. Big difference. "She's okay," I said.

"Just don't do anything I wouldn't do," said Sondra.

"Like be a supportive, generous, understanding friend?"

"Just consider yourself warned, Fringe," said Sondra. "Now, I'm ever so grateful for a Diet Coke, and would be forever in your debt for something to eat. And then you can put on that Ben Stiller movie you love so much."

"You mean *Zoolander*?" I asked, nearly drooling. "Wait, you're going to . . . watch *another* movie? With me?"

"Do I look like I have anything better to do?" she asked.

"Yeah, you totally do." Glamorous as hell in inky

skinny jeans, a pink satin cami, silver high-heeled sandals.

"I make it a rule to always look my best," replied Sondra. "That said, my evening is conspicuously free. I'm as shocked to say this as you'll be to hear it, Fringe: Tonight, you're all I've got."

I said, "Likewise." I went over to the DVD shelf, found my fave movie of all time, cued it up, made us sammies, and sat on the couch opposite Sondra, giddy as a middle school girl.

We hung out for hours. Peaches jumped from her couch to the coffee table, and then over to my couch, and then back to Sondra's as if she couldn't decide which flavor of human she liked best.

When she came over to me: "My lap is clearly more desirable than yours."

When Peaches returned to Sondra: "More like your lap leaves a lot to be desired."

Against her will, Sondra laughed—out loud and *hard*—at the movie, like, ten times.

No beer, no cigarettes, no talk about boys and bars. When Sondra left—after midnight—I was sorry to see her go. Not that I'd admit to it, under threat of death. We both knew we'd never pass another night like this. Free of witnesses, relaxed with each other. An evening in a parallel universe.

Peaches stayed up with me for a little longer. She lay on my chest on the couch. She cleaned her paws, and then she started to lick my neck, grooming me like a mother cat cleans her kitten. As much as I saw her as my child, I realized that Peaches had a protective maternal instinct, too. In every female creature, there was the part that wanted to be taken care of, and the part that wanted to take care of others.

I wondered if I'd ever not need to feel protected. Being Noel's girlfriend was like wearing an invisible shield at school. His Ruling Class status protected me from spurious attack. But for all the advantages of being connected to Noel, he himself hadn't done a heck of a lot to get me out of the scrapes I'd gotten myself into over the last year. In fact, looking back, I'd helped him with his problems a lot more than he'd helped me. His main contribution to my emotional well-being was the fact that he loved me, touched me, cared about my happiness. That might be the most any girl could expect from a boyfriend.

I would have enjoyed discussing such notions with Noel. But that was impossible. For all I knew, in the almost two months since we'd last seen each other, Noel had stopped caring about me. Could go two ways: (1) His feelings had changed, and he no longer gave a crap about me, or (2) Noel just assumed our relationship was so solid that talking regularly was unnecessary. Was my craving to connect with him a sign of my insecurity? Possibly. Or maybe I just wanted to hear his voice.

Zack might have some insight on the subject, I realized. The man's opinion. I kissed Peaches's fluffy face and carried her upstairs to my room. We curled up together on my bed, her whiskers brushing against my collarbone. We breathed in unison for twenty counts, and then I drifted off on a fur-lined cloud.

17

"Where's Stella?" I asked Rosalyn when I arrived at the Brick the next morning.

Rosalyn shrugged. "Don't know, don't care."

"You're in a great mood today," I said.

Again, the shrug. "I'm at work early after studying all night. What kind of mood should I be in?"

"Peppy?"

"Just back off," she said, a bit meanly. "I'm not in the mood to play waitress with you today. This is my real job, okay? I need it to pay for tuition and books and food, okay?"

"This is my real job, too," I said. I didn't add, *"Okay?"*

"You're slumming in the kitchen to get material for a college application essay."

How did she know about that? I scrambled for the last word, but Rosalyn moved along, busying herself, filling filters full of coffee grounds and stacking them to use throughout the day. Raul and Ramon had their toqued heads down, laboring over the grill, either actively ignoring me or genuinely busy. Jorge was in the pantry, checking stock. Charlie didn't work on Fridays. If Stella didn't show up, we'd be shorthanded.

I called her on her cell. She didn't answer. I flipped my phone closed and got to work. Even if it was just my summer job, I did care about it. Sort of. I cared about being decent at it, and I'd show Rosalyn just how much. For the next couple of hours, I was the Golden Waitress. Jorge said I was "on fire," which was overheard by Raul, who rushed at me with a bucket of water.

At noon, hours into the day's service, I wandered out of the kitchen, up the stairs and out on the stoop for a two-minute breather. The air outside was approximately five thousand degrees hotter than inside the air-conditioned club, so the breather was more like a gasper. Especially so when a big black limousine pulled up right outside the Brick. Brooklyn Heights certainly had its share of movie stars and superrich people. But you rarely saw a limousine that big navigating the narrow one-way streets.

A few kids in tennis whites, just arriving for their lessons, tried to peer through the blacked-out windows. When the rear door opened, the kids scattered. I watched Rupert Sandstone emerge from the cavernous backseat. He was in Casual Mogul attire: a gray summer-weight suit, dress shirt, no tie, permanent

Miami tan. I had to admit, he looked pretty spectacu-
lar. Commanding, confident, and stinking of money,
Sandstone was every inch the millionaire pinup that
Donald Trump wished he were.

He put on a pair of sunglasses and then leaned
over the limo's open door. He put his hand back inside the car, like he'd forgotten something, and when
he pulled it back out, a woman was attached.

Not just any woman.

Aghast, I watched them kiss. Stella's eyes only for
him. His only for her.

I swallowed hard and then slipped back into the
club, raced down the stairs to cower in the kitchen.

Rosalyn said, "That was more than two minutes."

I said, "Sorry."

"What's the matter with you?" she asked.

"Take your break now," I said, ignoring her
question.

Rosalyn shrugged and left the kitchen for parts
unknown. Stella strolled in seconds later, a dreamy
expression on her face.

Through the cutout window, I saw Jorge in the
dining room, greeting Rupert Sandstone, also just
arriving, and ushering him to a table for one.

Stella lazily put on an apron. She smiled at me
and said, " 'Sup?"

"Where have you been?" I asked. She glared at
me. "It's just been really busy. We needed you."

"Get used to being shorthanded," she said. "Rupert offered me a job, Dora. Singing in South Beach at his club. He'll start me in the piano bar. It's perfect for me. He's giving me a three-month contract! I'll live in the hotel and get paid a fortune. Eight shows a week. Take requests, do standards. Easy money."

"You slept with him," I said matter-of-factly.

"If I hadn't slept with him," she said, just as flatly, "he wouldn't have offered me the job."

"You can't be this naive," I said. "You're going to have to sleep with him *again*. And *again*."

Stella looked at me like I'd just grown a second head. "*I'm* naive?" she said. "You think I don't know exactly what I'm doing? Everyone has their own selfish agenda, in every relationship. People do what they have to do. Except you, right?"

I wasn't sure what she meant, but I said, "I do what I have to do."

"No, you don't," she said. "You don't even understand what I'm talking about."

Now she was making me feel stupid. "Everyone has to make difficult choices in life. . . ." I started.

But she interrupted me. "Besides, the fact is Rupert and I made a real human connection last night. I find him sexually attractive. He thinks of me as a talented performer with unlimited potential. His faith in me goes a long way toward my being attracted to him."

"Paging Dr. Freud," I said, interrupting her right back. "Looking for Daddy's approval much?"

Stella laughed, but I got the impression she didn't think my analysis was so funny. "You have no idea what it means to want something so bad that the wanting itself defines who you are," she said.

"You mean being a singer?" I asked.

"You really are completely clueless," said Stella, apparently disgusted that I failed to understand her cryptic message. "Just leave me alone. No more tagging along after me anymore."

And then she balled up the apron she'd just put on, threw it in the hamper and walked into the dining room. She went over to Sandstone's table. He smiled warmly at her. She said something. He glanced at the cutout window. I ducked and then peeked again. Stella was gone. Sandstone was saying something to Jorge, who frowned in response.

Rosalyn came up behind me. "Good riddance," she said. "It'll be a lot better around here without Stella."

"You're so sure she's not coming back?" I asked. "I bet she'll come to her senses in a day or two, walk back in here and apologize for insulting me, and admit she degraded herself."

"You really don't have a clue," said Rosalyn, shaking her head.

❀   ❀   ❀

I'd maligned Stella for expecting a man to solve her problems. And what was the first thing I did when I got out of the Brick? I sought out the only man in my life at the moment to try to solve my problems. Oh, sweet, bitter irony.

I found Zack at Friends, hours after closing time for the night. All the storefront window blinds were closed, and I couldn't see inside. I rang the clinic buzzer and called Zack's cell phone simultaneously. I saw movement between the spaces of the blinds. His eyes appeared, a phone pressed against his cheek. In my ear, he said, "Hey."

I said, "I'm upset," and then I burst into tears, standing on the street, holding the phone.

Zack let me in. I stumbled into the clinic waiting area and flopped down on the couch usually filled with eager adoptive families. Zack sat next to me and asked, "Did Peaches die?"

"No!" I said. "She's perfectly fine."

"Oh," he said. "Then why are you crying? And, if you don't mind, could you please stop?"

I filled him in about Stella and Rosalyn. How they'd collectively called me a naive, clueless rube. "The worst part about it is that they're right," I said. "I'm terrified about my future. I'm not prepared to do whatever needs to be done, like Stella. Or to suck all the fun out of life, like Rosalyn. I don't think my cynical optimism is going to get me into college, or

land me a real job or keep my boyfriend interested."
All my disjointed problems and worries suddenly
came to a head. "I'm unprepared," I continued. "I've
had the best education money can buy. I've done
whatever my teachers and my parents have asked
me to do. For seventeen years, I've been taught and
trained and guided to become a responsible person.
But the idea of actually being responsible for myself terrifies me! I'm freaking out! This is me, losing
my shit. On this couch. Which is covered in cat hair,
meanwhile."

Zack listened. He nodded and seemed sympathetic. I wasn't sure he caught every word, because
I was rambling. But he was alert and watched me
in an animal way, taking in my body language, listening to unspoken signals that only dogs—and hot
vets—could hear.

He said, "I don't think you're clueless."

"I am," I insisted.

"You're a compassionate, intelligent, beautiful
young woman," he said. "There's nothing wrong with
being scared about the future. It's part of life. And
it doesn't stop. Adults are scared about their future.
No one knows what's going to happen, one day to the
next."

"You're scared? I don't believe it," I said.

"Not today, but some days," he said. "A theoreti-
cal fear."

"Like the fear that you'll never meet a woman, fall in love, get married and have kids?" I asked.

He laughed. "I have had that fear," admitted Zack. "And others. I think it shows an impressive level of intellectual sophistication for you to see that in me."

"Oh yeah, I'm real sophisticated," I said. "I was the height of sophistication when I blew my nose in the floating pool."

Zack smiled reassuringly. "You really are okay, Dora."

Impulsively, I gave him a thank-you hug.

Which he returned.

The hug lasted longer than necessary. He started patting my back. The pats turned into strokes. The strokes into caresses. He shifted to pull me closer, and pressed against me. That was when I felt it.

Wood.

I flashed back to middle school dances when the boys would practically dry hump the girls. Not me, of course. I was standing against the wall with Eli and Liza, seething with bitterness and jealousy while mocking the writhing mass of bodies on the basketball court/dance floor.

But tonight, I was the one getting humped. By Zack. On my leg. Sort of the way a dog does it.

It would come as no surprise that this move wasn't sexy or a turn-on. The opposite, in fact. I took a deep breath and tried to think of a gentle discouragement.

Zack misinterpreted my inhale as excitement, and then kissed me on the lips.

I now knew, beyond a shadow of a doubt, that having a fantasy about a kiss did not mean that I'd enjoy the reality. I'd envisioned Zack looking at me with sexual craving. I'd imagined his lips pressed against mine. I'd even thought about his, ahem, wood. During these reveries, I'd felt a tingly, good sensation.

But that wasn't what I felt now. I'd describe my current reaction as repulsion. The hands on me were not Noel's. The lips on me were not soft and welcomed. This man, my boss, ten years older than me, had decided to maul me at a time of emotional tenderness. If that wasn't taking advantage, I'd pay to know what was.

Zack Gerritson was handsome, smart, caring to critters, an accredited doctor of veterinary medicine. But Zack Gerritson was also a cad.

I pushed him off. My years of Brownstone politeness training were called to the floor. When you didn't want what someone offered to you, what was the proper way to respond?

"No, thank you," I said, getting off the couch, backing up to the clinic door, slipping out onto Atlantic Avenue and running all the way home.

18

At not one point during those three minutes did I feel physically threatened. His kiss had been a lame attempt, not a violent assault. Sort of like shooting a ball at a basket with one arm and one leg, blind in both eyes, and hoping you'd score anyway. His face when I ran out of there: disappointed, embarrassed, hurt. Probably a mirror of my own expression. Funny how such a handsome face could be transformed by negative emotions. They took over his skin and bones, twisting him ugly. On the other hand, positive emotions on the face made anyone more attractive.

I made a mental note to smile more often.

But not tonight. I got home, found my apartment dark, empty, eerily quiet. I called for Peaches, like a desperate cry from a drowning woman.

"PEACHES!!!" I sobbed. "Where ARE YOU?"

Maybe I was being a tad melodramatic.

When I heard the padded thud of her paws coming down the stairs and into the dining room, I almost wept with joy. I wasn't completely alone. Peaches was here for me. She'd always be here for me. Zack, the masher, was a lousy kisser, and a lousy vet, as well. It'd been five days since I'd taken in Peaches. She hadn't slowed down or thrown up. By his estimate, she should have died by now.

I remembered, in my Googling, that a cat could be a carrier for feline leukemia and never succumb to the disease itself. So what if Peaches had bad teeth and bumps? Big honking deal.

Sweeping her up in my arms, I buried my damp face (it was ninety-two degrees, and I'd been running, and, you know, crying) in her soft fluff. It was calming, especially when she purred, her trademark deep, guttural declaration of happiness. She loved me. I loved her. Our love would last forever.

This was the reason people had pets. Unconditional affection on a two-way street. It was unthinkable that I hadn't had this relationship in my life before. My parents had seriously dropped the ball there.

I carried the precious bundle to my room, where I gently deposited her on my bed and then crumpled upon it to cry and cry, great buckets of pitiful tears.

I missed Noel, my friends, my parents. Even Joya.

In the ocean of independence, I was adrift. Fortunately, I was also tired. This bad day would end if I

fell asleep. I'd wake up with Peaches purring next to
me. She'd give me the courage to get back out there
and start again.

Or not. The next morning, I called in sick to the
Brick. I was sick, in the "sick and tired" sense. Since
nothing was going my way, I decided to take a little
time out, to assess what the hell was happening, and
why I had this penetrating bad feeling even though,
on the face of it, my life was pretty much fine. True,
the one friendship I'd made this summer crashed.
The boss I'd respected turned out to be a masher.
My boyfriend forgot I was alive. But that was only
part of the problem. I was pinned to my bed with an
overwhelming sense of anticipatory dread. It was a
strange sensation, like the worst was yet to come, and
that it was surely coming soon.

Hiding out at home was, clearly, the only thing to
do. I puttered. Rearranged my closet. Poured sweat.
Watered Dad's wilting container garden. Emptied and
deflated the pool. I started to relax, to feel safe. If I
stayed huddled in my sanctuary, no harm could come.

But something did come. Or, I should say,
some*one*.

Around two in the afternoon, the apartment
buzzer sounded, staccato and loud. Peaches jerked
out of a sound sleep, leapt in fright off the bed and
onto the sweater shelf.

"Hello?" I asked the intercom.

"It's Rosalyn," she said.

I buzzed her in.

As soon as she entered my apartment, she said, "Oh, Christ, I forgot about the heat up here."

"Want a drink?" I asked.

"Water is fine," she said, and followed me into the kitchen. Taking a paper towel from the roll, Roz wiped her brow and the back of her neck. "Did you blow off work because of what I said yesterday?" she asked.

Gotta love blunt. "No," I said.

"Bullshit," she said.

"Not just you," I said. "Stella was harsh, too."

"So you got your feelings hurt."

"It was my fault? I asked for it?" I asked.

Rosalyn said, "Just . . . learn to take it a little, okay? I'm sorry I hurt your feelings. We need you at the Brick. Get dressed."

"I'm not going," I said, resolute. "You can't make me."

Okay, even I knew I sounded like a bratty kid. But I wanted my day off. I'd been working almost every day for seven weeks, at two jobs, and going out at night, too.

Rosalyn said, "Okay, whatever. Stay here and stew in your pajamas. It won't make you feel better. The only thing that'll help is going to work, being around people and accomplishing something. Laziness breeds itself, Dora."

"I'm not lazy," I said, "I'm depressed."

"Depression, same thing," she said. "You need to pull yourself out of it."

I knew she meant well, and that her bootstraps philosophy of life made sense to her. "Look, Roz, I'm not motivated like you. I'm a spoiled, selfish, emotionally vulnerable person. I feel things deeply. And right now, I feel, deeply, like I need to take a day to myself. You must get that way sometimes. You're not a machine."

Rosalyn stared at me like my skin had turned green. "Of course I feel that way," she boomed. "But I force myself to get over it, and I go on."

"One day, you'll snap," I said.

"What makes you think I haven't snapped already?" she asked. "I've been broken."

"Heartbroken?" I asked, suddenly revived by the hint of a romantic adventure in Rosalyn's past, and her upcoming emotional confession. "You never talk about boys, so I assumed you were . . . inexperienced."

"I'm twenty, Dora," she said.

"And you don't want to get pregnant young, like your mother," I said. "I thought you chanted that like a mantra every night to kill your sex drive."

"I do," she said. Realizing how funny that sounded,

she said, "Not literally. Look, I don't want to talk about this. Just take my word for it. My ex-boyfriend didn't turn out to be worth sacrificing my future for. Far from it. No man is worth that. At least, none I've met so far. The men I meet tell me to wear shorter skirts and higher heels. They think being pretty should be my one and only goal in life. That's fine for Stella, but not for me. She quit today, by the way." Roz drained her glass. "Enough of this. Are you coming to the Brick or not?"

"Not," I said.

She put her empty glass on the counter. "I'm going," she said.

"Wait," I said.

Rosalyn smiled. "Change your mind?"

"When Stella quit, did she ask about me?"

Shaking her head in disbelief, Roz said, "You're incredible."

"Did she?" I repeated.

Opening the apartment door, Roz said, "Nope."

"Number sixty-eight," said the woman giving out wristbands at the floating pool. It was 8:30 p.m., the last swim of the day. After brooding at home for twenty-four hours straight, I had to get outside, and what could be more purifying—in the physical and karmic sense—than submerging myself in the cleansing, chlorinated waters I associated with Stella and Zack? One dunk, and their memories would be washed from my mind.

Eager to begin the process, I rushed through the locker room and onto the patio. A lot of people were already in the pool. I caught sight of a couple that looked familiar. No, couldn't be them.

Blinking a few times, I looked closer, took a few steps forward to confirm. Seated on the pool edge, a strawberry blonde kicked her slim legs in the water. She wore a sexy crochet bikini I'd never seen before. Her hair was loose and wet, slicked back and shiny on her head like a seal. Following the line of her long limb, I spied the man bobbing in the water at her feet. He smiled at her, bedazzled, and grabbed one of her ankles. She giggled and fluttered him loose. He smiled charmingly at her, said something that made her slide into the water, into his waiting arms.

Stella Walters and Zack Gerritson. They were together. Laughing. Touching. I watched, frozen on the patio. And then I gagged. Had I actually puked, it would have been spectacular. See, I'd eaten quite a bit of food that day in the boredom of my sequestration. I'd kind of cleaned out the fridge with a fork.

"Hey! You in the green! No gagging on the patio!" squawked the lifeguard with the bullhorn.

A hundred pairs of eyes turned my way. Including Zack's and Stella's.

Seeing them see me, I immediately turned around

to leave. But I stopped myself. No. I would not run away. This conversation had to happen. If I chickened out, I'd be tormented by my cowardice for weeks. Possibly months. Maybe forever.

I turned around, walked toward their bobbing heads in the pool. They looked up at me, seemingly concerned.

"What the fuck do we have here?" I asked.

"Hey! You in the green! No cursing!"

Stella pulled herself out of the water. "Dora, it's not what you think."

That was highly unlikely. I said, "You guys don't even know each other! Don't tell me this is a crazy coincidence."

"I can tell you're upset to see us together," she said. "Although I don't really understand why. Zack is your boss, right? And you have a boyfriend, right?"

Good question(s). What disgusted me so much about seeing them together? Only yesterday, Zack had forcibly shoved his tongue in my mouth. Only yesterday, Stella dumped me because I'd questioned her "genuine" attraction to an old man. Both had betrayed me in different ways. And now they were doing it as an entwined pair, glomming all over each other in *my corner* of the pool. The pool I'd brought them to. How long had they been seeing each other behind my back?

Zack said to me, "Stella came looking for *you* at

the animal clinic to apologize. She told me you guys had an argument. I told her that you and I hadn't parted on such good terms, either."

"So you decided to come to *my corner* of *my pool*, and glom all over each other?" I asked him. "Did you tell her that you put the D.V.M. moves on me last night? That I'd come to you when I was upset, and you practically sucked my face off? That I ran away from you—*screaming*?"

Stella looked questioningly at Zack, who must not have mentioned what happened last night at the clinic. I added, "I would never fool around with a guy almost twice my age. Unlike you, Stella. Actually, Sandstone might be three times your age. What happened to your love connection with him anyway? Are you still moving to Miami, or is that over, too?"

Zack looked at her. Apparently, she hadn't mentioned any of her plans to him.

I felt slimy in the presence of these two liars, opportunists and betrayers. A wave of contempt rose up my throat, and I had to get it out. "You know, Stella, you're not a great singer. You're slightly above average. Even if you slept with a hundred rich old men, starving kids in Africa will never know your name."

Turning to Zack, I said, "And you! Forget for a second that you pounced on a teenage girl when she was crying on your couch—which might be illegal; I'll have to check with my lawyer—you're a lousy vet!

Peaches is the healthiest, happiest cat I've ever seen, and you were twenty seconds from killing her. How many other healthy cats have you murdered? How can you sleep?"

Zack looked like I'd kicked him in the bathing suit. Stella stared at the surface of the water. I wondered if her shame was for how she'd treated me, Sandstone, Zack or herself. Could be all of the above. I couldn't believe I'd ever looked up to her, envied her, been awed by her powers of seduction. She was a needy, hungry, desperate, confused slacker. I was just as disgusted that I'd trusted Zack, fantasized about him, used him to forget about Noel's neglect.

Nothing more to say; I'd already said too much. I went back to the locker room, exited the "beach," and walked up Joralemon Street to Garden Place, my beach towel flapping behind me like a cape, my flip-flops slapping the pavement.

I destroyed those people, I thought. I'd unleashed a torrent of venom. I'd assassinated their souls. They both deserved it. I should've felt proud of myself for doing what needed to be done. And yet I couldn't help feeling like I'd assassinated a little bit of my own soul, too.

19

To make matters worse, when I got home, the door to our apartment was ajar.

Had I left it open? I didn't think so. And the lights were on. I was sure I hadn't left them on, because it was just dusk when I set out for the pool. Door open, lights on. Could mean only one thing: We were being robbed.

I tiptoed/flip-flopped back down the stairs and out to the stoop. Flipping open my cell phone, I had to catch my breath before dialing.

The 911 operator got right to the point. "What is your emergency?" she asked.

"My apartment is being robbed!" I shouted the street address a few times.

"Is there anyone in the apartment?"

"Just the robbers," I said. "My parents aren't home. They left me here in Brooklyn to fend for myself while they gallivanted all over New England," I said. "Not that I'm resentful about being deserted by my own flesh and blood. No, they should have their fun. I'll stay behind to sweat in this oven of an apartment, and deal with random break-ins."

"Please hold," she said. "I'll connect you to children's services to report parental abandonment."

"No!" I said. "I'm seventeen. Not exactly child services material. It's not like my parents chained me to a radiator. At least, not lately."

Pause. "Is that a joke?" asked the operator.

"Not funny, I'm guessing?"

"Are you in a safe place?"

I glanced up and down my streetlight-illuminated, quiet block. I'd heard about a robbery here and there over the years. Never on Garden Place. We had a neighborhood watch. The signs were everywhere.

"Are the cops coming?" I asked.

"Police are on their way," said the operator. "Do you require further assistance?"

"Probably," I said.

She hung up. Within a minute, I heard a siren. The good thing about living in an upscale neighborhood? Excellent police response. A cop car pulled up to my building, lights spinning, bouncing off buildings, and two huge, beefy, burly, mustachioed uniformed cops got out. With guns, hats, walkie-talkies, utility belts and everything.

I said, "Over here! This is the place."

The more massive cop looked at my bikini and beach towel and asked, "Describe the scene, miss."

Miss. I liked that. "I came home and the door was open, the lights were on. I'm SURE I closed the door behind me. Someone is up there. I just know it."

"No one else lives in the apartment?" he asked, drawing his weapon (!!!).

"My sister and parents," I said. "But my sister is at camp, and my parents are on vacation."

The cops grunted the secret language of law enforcement at each other. A bunch of numbers and letters. Code. I watched a lot of *Law & Order*, to be sure, but this live show was far more exciting.

"We'll go up," said the spokescop. "Wait here. Make sure no one steals the car."

A joke? From a cop? He might've smiled under the mustache.

I let them in the building's two front doors. Then I waited on the stoop. Although the police car lights were lulling and pretty to behold, I would have rather watched the capture of the evildoers who'd invaded the sanctuary of home.

I waited for the sound of shots fired. Nothing. I counted to a hundred. Nothing. Deciding to risk it, I let myself into the building lobby. Still hearing nothing, I climbed the stairs, one flight, two flights, until I was on the landing of our apartment.

I crept toward the door. It was still slightly ajar. In my heart, I feared the cops had been subdued by the desperate invaders. The urge to flee hit me hard across the midsection. I bravely continued toward the door anyway, and nudged it open with the toe of my shoe. In the movie version of this scene, the audience would be screaming, "Do. Not. Go. In. There!"

The door swung open. Enough for me to stick my head in. I peeked down the short hallway into our dining room.

There, at the table where I've eaten countless meals, I saw the invaders. They were seated at the table, mugs of coffee in their mitts, the two policemen standing over them. The shock of seeing them turned my knees to jelly.

"Dora? Is that you?"

"Hi, Dad," I said sheepishly, stepping into the hallway, calculating how much trouble I was in now.

"We came back early to surprise you," said Mom.

"Surprise," said Dad.

The spokescop asked, "Are these your parents?"

"Otherwise known as the mortgage holders, yeah," I said.

The smaller (but still huge) police dude grunted some code to his partner.

"We still have to make a report," said the designated talker of the pair. "And might as well do a sweep of the place, just to be sure."

While New York's Finest went about their business, I gave Mom and Dad tentative hugs, and then bashfully pulled up a chair at the table. "It's days like these that you feel blessed to have had children," I said.

"Didn't you see the Volvo?" asked Mom. "We got a spot right across the street."

Actually, I had seen it, and thought, "Wow, that car looks exactly like ours!"

"This is a first for me," said Dad. "Being busted by cops in my own home, while in the john."

He used the word "john" for bathroom. Didn't know why. I assumed he once knew someone named John and didn't like him very much.

Mom said, "It's convenient, actually, because we thought of calling the cops about you."

"Me?"

"We e-mailed you several times and left messages, and you didn't call back," said Mom. "Then we got home and the place was empty and smelling a bit . . . funky. We got scared."

I sniffed the air. Ah, the distinct eau du litter box, unscooped for a day or two.

"Mom, Dad, I'm sorry about not calling you back or e-mailing. I was very caught up in my own life," I said.

"Who says teenagers are inconsiderate?" said Dad.

"I'm sorry about calling the cops, too, but if you look at it objectively, you have to acknowledge that it makes sense. I'd been gone for only a half an hour. The door was open, the lights were on." I would have to tell them about Peaches eventually, that I'd adopted a pet without permission. To soften them up, I said, "I missed you guys, so so sososososo much!"

Dad guffawed. "What, did you run out of food?"

The cops came down the stairs, checked the deck quickly and thereby concluded their search.

I asked, "Does this kind of thing happen often?"

"All the time," said the talker.

"How often?"

"Once a year," he said. "You've just helped us reach our quota."

On their way out, Dad held the door for them, and said he donated annually to the Policemen's Benevolent Association. They seemed grateful.

"Well, I suppose we could see this as a good sign," said Dad, closing the door behind them before reclaiming his chair. "If you were drinking and smoking pot, you wouldn't have called the police over to investigate."

Mom said, "The bright side is that she's not breaking the law."

Dad shrugged. "I'll bet she's not smuggling diamonds, either. Not in her bathing suit anyway."

"Dad!" I screamed. "You're disgusting."

"Been swimming?" asked Mom, noticing my getup and the beach towel, still hung over my shoulders.

"Yup, swimming," I said. "In over my head."

"Figuratively?" asked Mom.

I sighed, heavy, wet, full of spit and meaning. "Okay, I've figured out the difference between being a high school senior—*rising*—and a fully fledged independent adult."

"Twenty years and thirty pounds?" said Dad.

"When you're in high school, there's no escape from the people around you. You have to see them every day for at least a year. So your actions have consequences," I said. "You have to live with your mistakes."

"Adults don't have to live with their mistakes?" asked Mom.

"No!" I said. "They don't! They can just quit their job and move to Miami. They can behave like jerks, knowing they'll never see the people they mistreat again!" As soon as I said it, I realized 90 percent of my anger was about Stella. And yet I'd called Zack Gerritson a murderer. Pang of guilt. Sort of. He had macked on me, only to go after Stella one day later.

"Adults can do one thing on Monday and the opposite on Tuesday. If you don't get caught, then you can do anything you want, regardless of whether it's right or fair. Whatever satisfies your desires at the moment."

Mom and Dad stared at me for a few beats. Then they glanced furtively at each other. The words "satisfies" and "desires" raised the red flag for them. Mom said, "What exactly are you talking about, Dora? And what does this have to do with swimming?"

"I'm not talking about *me*," I said.

"Who are you talking about?" asked Mom.

I opened my mouth and then closed it. Should I tell them? I wondered. Would I come off badly? Had I brought any of the last week on myself? Mom and Dad, best-selling authors of *His-and-Her Seduction*, were strong believers in the power of thoughts, and I definitely had thoughts about Zack. Of course, there was a world of difference between thoughts and actions. I'd kept my actions under control. He hadn't. I wasn't at fault.

I told them. Skipping all the nights of drinking with Stella and the actual kiss with Zack. I said he'd "come on to me," but didn't mention actual touching. When I finished, describing word for word what I'd said to them at the pool, I waited for Mom and Dad to congratulate me on standing up for myself.

But they didn't. Mom said, "You owe both of them an apology."

"*What???*"

Dad agreed. "You should do it in person, tomorrow."

"But they were horrible to me!" I said.

Mom said, "Okay, now I'm going to tell you the difference between a high school kid and a fully fledged independent adult."

"Ready," I said.

"High school kids view other people's selfish behavior as something done to them," said Mom. "Adults are just living their lives, trying not to be lonely and broke, and, when they're brave enough, taking opportunities when they come."

Dad said, "Allow me to clarify what Mom is trying to say. . . ."

"I got it, Dad."

"Permit me to elaborate," he said.

"No need," I said.

"What your mother means," he persisted, "is that you haven't yet learned not to take things personally."

"Learning not to care," I said.

Dad said, "Sort of! It's more like objectivity. Stella's taking this Miami job; it's got nothing to do with you, Dora. You might think she's making a mistake. And you might be right. Who knows? But as far as Stella is concerned, it's none of your business. As a friend, she wanted support from you. You judged her and criticized her, and then, at the pool, you outright insulted her. And you expect her to feel bad that she's offended your sensibilities?"

"Okay, stop," I said. "Really, stop now."

Mom continued. "And the vet. He's obviously a lonely person, grasping for companionship. He surrounds himself with animals in lieu of actual people. Stella is a naturally seductive person—I saw that for myself. To Zack, she must've looked like a long drink of water to a thirsty man. And he was coming off the humiliation of misreading your signals, and the disgrace of hitting on a teenager. And he should be ashamed of himself! Propositioning a child! If he laid a finger on you, Dora, I'd go down there and give him a piece of my mind!"

Dear God. "Not a big piece."

"One thing makes no sense," said Dad. "Why did you call this vet a murderer? It's not murder to put down a suffering animal. It's humane, and I'm sure it's the worst part of his job. He should be applauded for doing it."

I'd also left out the part about Peaches. My strategy was to tell them how I'd been wronged in their absence so they'd be more sympathetic about my adopting the cat. As it turned out, they were far from sympathetic. They thought I'd been wrong, not wrong*ed*.

Tactical error.

Dad said, "Why do you look funny?"

Mom said, "And what *smells* funny?" She crinkled her nostrils.

Dad cocked his head. "Yes, the stench is getting worse by the minute. Is it . . . ammonia? And ripe—rotting—*something*. Maybe a mouse died in the walls? Or a piece of food rolled under the fridge? I'll just follow my nose."

He stood up. Sniffed the air. The litter box was in the closet under the stairs. No more than ten feet from where he was.

"I have other news," I blurted. "I was afraid to tell you before."

Mom groaned. "What'd you break?"

I moved to the closet door and opened it. The aroma burst forth like a toxic cloud. Mom and Dad instantly recoiled, as if punched.

"I adopted a cat," I said.

And then they swooned, as if the double whammy of stink and news was too much for their consciousness.

I said, "Zack was going to euthanize Peaches, but I felt an instant connection to her—hard to explain— so I begged him to let me bring her home and care for her for the few days she had left. But it's been a week, and she's alive and kicking. I just knew she wasn't really sick. Zack was two inches away with the syringe to kill her. I saved her life."

I took a deep breath after my speech. Mom and Dad were still stunned silent. "Come upstairs," I said. "As soon as you meet her, you'll love her! She's the sweetest cat on earth, and I'll take care of her all by myself, as I have been, all week long. Plus, this'll please you, I'm sure I'll study harder and get better grades with her on my bed. She helps me concentrate. Pets lower blood pressure—I'm sure you've read that. . . ."

"Dora, be quiet," said Mom, rubbing her forehead. To Dad, she said, "We drove three hundred miles for this?" To me, she said, "You had no business adopting a pet without discussing it with us first."

"Let's not make any snap decisions, Gloria," he said.

"There're no decisions to make!" I said. "Peaches is mine. I love her, she loves me, and I'm keeping her." I started to tear up. "It would be insanely cruel of you to even suggest Peaches couldn't stay. It's incomprehensible. It'd be like child abuse."

"Really, Dora, shut up," said Mom, getting angry now. For a small woman, she had a large temper.

Dad, forever the peacemaker, said, "Why don't we meet Peaches?"

"She's probably asleep on my sweater shelf," I said. "It's unbearably cute, how she snuggles up in the cashmere."

"And gets hair all over them," groused Mom.

"Just wait right here," I said, and sprinted up the stairs to my room.

Peaches was exactly where I expected to find her, on my sweater shelf, curled up like a fur ball.

I listened for the sound of her purring—which she did, even when she was asleep—but my heart was pounding too loud. I reached up and stroked her on the back. Weirdly, she didn't lean into my hand, like she always did, even when she was sleeping.

I drew my hand back, instinctively, as if I'd been scalded by boiling water. The reality of what had happened hit my body before my conscious mind. My spine chilled, and that made me flop sweat. A wave a nausea hit me, too, and I ran to the bathroom. As I heaved into the toilet, I was thinking, "Peaches is sure acting funny." My brain refused to accept what my body already understood plainly.

Willful ignorance. I didn't want to comprehend the truth, and therefore didn't. For a few minutes anyway.

My parents heard me yakking in the bathroom. They bounded up the stairs.

"Dora, my God, what's wrong?" asked Mom, standing in the bathroom doorway.

From my bedroom, I heard Dad call softly, "Gloria, you'd better come in here."

I lifted my head high enough to watch her go. Then I heard her sharp intake of breath, some muttering back and forth between Mom and Dad, then the faint sound of scuffling, and Dad's heavy footsteps going downstairs.

In a kneel, I flushed. Mom was back in the

bathroom threshold. Her face was gray beneath her vacation tan.

I said, "Why does Dad call it a 'john'?"

"Sweetheart," said Mom gently, reaching out to help me to my feet.

Mom's paws are tiny, smaller than mine, had been for years. She was just this petite person, but with the emotional strength of a thousand men. She'd never backed away from difficult feelings; she confronted them head on. And here she was, ready, willing and able to help me, her firstborn daughter, mourn the loss of my first pet.

I guess I had the emotional strength of a gnat. Taking Mom's hand, I let her lift me up, and then I crumpled into her, more like slumped over her. She led me to her bedroom, where I collapsed on the queen-sized bed. Mom patted my shoulders, brushed back my hair, made small, circular comforting motions on my back.

The thing about crying inconsolably? Hiccups are guaranteed, as well as dehydration, blotchy skin, a headache; but there is also a fantastic, out-of-body feeling of exhilaration for having so much raw emotion. Granted, the emotion was bad. But it was true and pure, and its clarity swept away from my head the mess of Stella and Zack.

I felt a shift on the bed. Dad was on my other side now.

"What did you do with her?" I asked him.

"She's in a box in the hallway," he said gently. "I made some calls to see what to do next."

"We're burying her," I declared.

"Okay," said Dad calmingly. "But we don't have anywhere to do it."

"In your container garden," I said. "Some of the troughs are big enough." And some of the flowers were just as dead.

"That's not a very practical idea," said Dad.

"Why not? Won't the body be good fertilizer?" I asked. I was a bit demented with grief at this point. Suburban families had all the dirt in the world to bury their dead pets. Some of them probably had whole pet graveyards. An unexpected drawback to city living: no convenient place to inter.

Mom said, "I'm sure that would be a health hazard, Dora."

"I know," I said, rolling over, lying flat on my back with my hands over my face. "I'll take Peaches to the Friends clinic tomorrow morning for cremation. They have a service. Nominal fee. Urns available on request; otherwise, cardboard box."

Mom said, "I'd be happy to take her, if you're not up for it."

"We all know I have to do it by myself," I said, exhaling deeply and sitting up. "Obviously, I owe Zack an even bigger apology than I already owed him

from before. He was right about Peaches being sick.
I didn't want to believe it."

Mom said, "On some level, you probably knew
all along."

I nodded. I'd vacillated between wishing he'd
been wrong, fearing he'd been right and deluding
myself that my care and love would magically cure
her.

Dad asked, "Are you going to cry again? Because
I can get a towel from the closet."

Indeed, behind me on the blue bedspread there
was a softball-sized dark tear splotch, slowly spread-
ing.

"Oh yeah," I warned, voice warbling. "More tears
coming right up."

Dad fetched me a hand towel.

20

"You're not scheduled to work today," stated Donna Snagg when I walked into Friends early the next morning.

"You never liked me," I said, sensing her hostility, feeling upset again. Couldn't she see that my eyes were red from crying all night? Couldn't she smell the decomposing body of Peaches? I'd carried her body back to the clinic in the same cardboard pet carrier I'd taken her out of here in. That time, she'd been cushioned with a towel. This time, she was wrapped in a garbage bag, tied tightly on top, but the smell, in the heat, seeped out regardless.

Donna said, "I never . . . I have no opinion of you, one way or the other."

"That's a lie," I said. "It's impossible not to form an opinion."

"It's not only possible," she said, glancing at the carrier, detecting the smell. "It's recommended. For anyone who wants to hold on to their job."

I shifted the box to my other hand. "Are you threatening me?" Man, was I feeling defensive. I'd have called out a ninety-year-old grandma if she gave me the hairy eyeball.

Donna said, "I'm trying to give you some advice, Dora. You can take it or leave it. I don't really care."

"That's your secret?" I asked. "Not caring about anyone or anything?"

Donna ignored the dangling bait. "What brings you here on your day off?" she asked.

Uh, dead cat in box? "Is Zack here?" I asked.

"He's in his office," she said.

I went in back, lugging Peaches, who, despite ascending to cat heaven, was still very heavy. I took a moment, gathered my thoughts, replayed my speech. Then I knocked on Zack's door.

"Come in," he said.

To say he was surprised to see me would be the understatement of the year. When I pushed the door open and walked into the room, his green eyes bugged. Then he spilled his coffee. On his keyboard. Jumped up from his chair, knocking it over, frightening a dog that cowered in the corner.

"It's me," I said, declaring the obvious. "I've come back with my tail between my legs, as it were." Hmm, going by Zack's horrified expression, perhaps I shouldn't have mentioned any nether body parts. "I'm sorry. It was wrong to call you a murderer. And who you hook up with is none of my business. I wish you and Stella every happiness."

At this point, the beagle in the corner had regained composure, and was instantly enthralled by the ripe smell coming out of the cat carrier on the floor. He sniffed the box and growled low.

Zack said, "Is that . . . Peaches?"

A lump popped into my throat. I said, "Yes," and then started crying AGAIN. It astonished me that one person could expel so much liquid through the ducts, for so long. I babbled through the tears, "She died last night. You were right about her. In hindsight, I see that she was slowing down for the last two days. Sleeping more. Eating less. And then she went to sleep in my closet and didn't wake up. All things considered, it was a pretty good way to go. I still think it was the right decision to bring her home and let her die in a warm nest of cashmere than for her to get a shot and croak on a cold steel table."

He nodded, sympathetic and unhinged by a crying female. "Have you given any thought to what you'd like to do with the body?"

"Cremation," I said.

Zack said, "I'll call our service in Park Slope. They'll come pick up . . . the box . . . and deliver the ashes tomorrow morning. Would you like to look at their selection of urns?"

He was all business, not taking our recent past

into account at all during this conversation. It was both weird and easy. Better to deal with logistics than sticky personal stuff. Which could have been a wise approach to working here, in a macro sense. But it was too late for that. I was a customer now. Not an employee.

"The porcelain urn is fine," I said. "And then I want you to send the package to Peaches's owner. The old woman who moved to the assisted-living home. They might object to pets, but they can't have a problem with ashes."

"Dora, that's a lovely idea," he said. "Perhaps you might be willing to write her a note."

I reached into my purse and withdrew a sealed envelope. "Already done," I said, handing the letter to Zack. "Pay for it all with the money you owe me. I won't be coming back to pick up my last paycheck. If it's not enough, send a bill. You know where I live."

I'd stayed up late into the night writing the story of the last week of Peaches's life to a woman I'd never met, who was likely to die soon herself. Like I said, I cried a lot, pouring my thoughts and sadness onto the page, writing a eulogy for an animal that meant a lot to me, but even more to someone else. It felt good, earthy, to do it. The old woman probably wouldn't care about Stella, Rosalyn and Zack, but I wanted, needed, to write the whole story, describe everyone Peaches came into contact with, and the context of the meetings.

While writing, it occurred to me that something died for me this summer besides my first pet. I thought of it as the death of the illusion of control. You might believe you had control over your own life, and the people in it, their actions and your own. But that was an illusion. A dream wrapped up in smoke. The truth was, you have no control. Which wasn't necessarily a bad thing. No one else had control, either. And life would be a little boring if you always knew how it was going to turn out.

"You have this woman's address?" I asked Zack, just to be sure (and a bit controlling; some habits died hard).

"I have her son's contact info," said Zack. "Don't worry, Dora. I'll get the package to the right place."

I nodded, wiped my cheeks, patted the top of the carrier, whispered a few parting words into the air hole (nearly fainting from the smell). I smiled at Zack. He smiled back, big eyes pained. He said nothing, though, so I left.

I thought he'd call after me, apologize for . . . whatever he might feel bad about, if anything. But he didn't. No closure for me there. No words of regret about Stella or kissing me. Or Peaches's sudden death.

What could he have said that would've satisfied

me? That the heat made him go crazy? That he was so hard up, he would have kissed anyone he could catch? That he was like his animals, operating on instinct, attending to base needs of food, sleep, humping.

Or maybe his reticence about what had happened between us said what words couldn't. That there was nothing worth mentioning, no understanding or mutual appreciation, anymore. And if there had been once, it'd been silenced, rendered mute; no language existed to describe the loss. I sympathized with speechless animals, their inability to talk or express themselves with words. Zack had offered me big, sad puppy eyes only. I left them behind as I walked out of there, my own eyes trained forward.

21

Peaches's death, and the emotional downward spiral that followed, altered my perception of reality. It was as if I'd taken a hefty dose of a recreational drug called Agony. The people and places were familiar, but the feeling of disheartened numbness? That was new.

I returned to the Brick the next day. It was like returning to my distant past, although it had been only two days since I'd last worked there. My apology to Zack had been genuine, and I still owed a few groveling words to Stella. I'd tried her cell phone, and called her at her parents'. She hadn't returned either call. I hoped she'd be at the Brick when I showed.

"Stella? For all I know, she's already in Miami," said Jorge.

I knew she was in Brooklyn two nights ago. At the pool. Perhaps I should call Zack to track down Stella. Right after I jumped in front of an oncoming subway train.

I tied on my apron, and started cracking shells for "egg goo"—a milk/egg blended mixture we kept in vats for omelets. Charlie was setting up tables for the brunch service. A new waitress, Linda, older than Rosalyn, was helping Charlie. She seemed nice. Friendly. I smiled and introduced myself, the whole time thinking, Whatever.

I'd learned the meaning of the word "desultory" for SAT prep. Basically, it meant "not giving a shit." As such, my work at the Brick for the remainder of the day, and the next day, and the day after that, was desultory as hell. Ironically, I'd never had more efficient shifts, made fewer mistakes or as much in tips. The paradox was striking. The less I cared, the better I did.

Was this my future? Was success in the working world really a measure of how little you cared about the work you were doing? I'd always strived to put my full heart and mind into my relationships, schoolwork (when it was interesting) and friendships.

On the third day at the Brick, post-Stella, post-Peaches, I asked Rosalyn, "Is it kind of boring here without her?"

"Who?" asked Roz.

"Stella."

"You're not really telling me you miss her," she said.

"I do," I said. I missed some passion in the kitchen. Her spark of excitement and energy.

Rosalyn said, "I guess I miss her a little, too. She definitely breathed some life into this place."

"How can you stand it?" I asked. "Coming here day after day, serving unappreciative people the same meals, doing a job you don't care about and never will?"

"I've told you a million times, Dora," said Roz, losing patience with me, which she'd also done a million times. "I've got dreams bigger than this restaurant. But I've got to start somewhere."

At the end of the shift, Jorge made an announcement. "People. Gather round. Mr. Sandstone sent me an e-mail last night, detailing some changes he wants to make at the restaurant," he said.

I asked, "He wants to have us work fewer hours for more money?"

"I knew this was going to happen," said Jorge, frowning. "As soon as you relax and let yourself think everything is okay, you get the curveball to the groin."

"Just tell us," asked Rosalyn, skeptical, aware of Jorge's overblown pessimism.

"Sandstone wants to renovate the restaurant. Top to bottom. The design of the dining room, the menu, the uniforms, the pricing. Wholesale remodeling."

Rosalyn clicked her tongue. Raul and Ramon looked at each other grimly. Charlie said, "Shit." Only newbie Linda seemed unfazed.

"God knows why," said Jorge, "but Sandstone has got it in his head to model the Brick restaurant on Craft Bar, some place in Manhattan. And he wants to hire a chef from some TV show."

"*Top Chef*?" I asked.

Jorge nodded. "I never even heard of it. Sandstone wrote, 'Find a *Top Chef* contestant who made it into the final four.' If anyone has the slightest idea what that means, tell me now, before I shoot myself."

I swallowed hard. So Stella *was* in Miami, whispering her ideas into Sandstone's head, unwittingly affecting the real lives of real people.

"When?" I asked.

"Sandstone has already hired an architect," said Jorge. "She's coming in tomorrow to meet with me. He wants to start renovations as soon as possible. In the best of all possible worlds, reopen in January." He paused. "I don't expect anyone to wait, but if you do, there's a job for you. That is, if I'm still here to hire you. As of August fifteenth, we're officially closed."

Raul and Ramon were already talking to each other in rapid Spanish. Jorge interjected a few comments in Spanish, which I didn't catch. Rosalyn calmly listened to their conversation, occasionally nodding but keeping quiet.

I asked, "Sandstone is willing to close the restaurant for months? He'll lose all that revenue."

Jorge said, "He'll make it back, and much more.

The new restaurant will be open to the general public. Not just club members. Part of the renovation is to put the entrance street-side."

Also Stella's ideas. Sandstone, obviously a smart business man, couldn't be willing to spend so much money and risk the loss of revenue if he didn't think her vision of the Brick would be a hit.

Sandstone had given her more credit than I had. He was, perhaps, the first person in Stella's life to take her seriously. No wonder she ran away with him. She'd said they had a genuine understanding. But if that were true, what was she doing with Zack in the pool?

I would have to add that to my list of Questions I'd Never Get Answered, along with Why Do Bad Things Happen to Good People?, Why Can Some People Eat and Eat and Never Gain Weight?, and How Does H&M Make Such Cute Clothes for Bargain Prices?

Linda—I never learned her last name—said, "Well, if it's okay with you, Mr. Mendez, I'm going to start looking for a new job tomorrow. No point staying here for just two weeks."

Jorge nodded grimly, and worked out the details about where to send her last check.

Rosalyn waited for Linda to leave before she asked, "You, too, Dora? Going to jump off the sinking ship?"

Everyone in the kitchen turned to look at me. Only Charlie seemed sympathetic. Simply by asking the question, Rosalyn had essentially defined me as disloyal, as not caring. We hadn't become close friends, true. We were just too different. But I wanted her to think of me as a decent human being, at the very least.

"I'm here until the bitter end," I declared. "And you're officially on my kill list for thinking I'd bail."

Jorge visibly relaxed. "Thank you, Dora. And thank all of you. I'm sorry this had to happen now. Just when things were starting to really hum."

Rosalyn said, "I'm sorry, Dora. It was defensiveness talking."

"You are aggressively defensive," I said.

"Am I still on your kill list?" she asked.

"Nah," I said. "I'll let you live. For now."

She gave me a weak grin in return. The other Mendezes were not in smiley moods. In this sea of dejection, I felt an emotional lift (why was I always so *contrary*?). I got the idea, on a wave of optimism (albeit cynical), that the future would be bright. Not just for me, but all of us. I can't say where it came from. But there it was.

"Come on, people," I said. "It's not all bad."

"Yeah, it is," said Ramon, in accented English.

"Let's discuss it over drinks," I said, going to the

refrigerator in back, and bringing forth two bottles of our cheapish mimosa champagne.

"Great idea!" said Charlie, grinning at me.

Jorge said, "Those are for paying customers, Dora." But he was smiling, giving me the go-ahead with a wink.

I fumbled with the wire around the cork. Rosalyn sighed with exasperation. "Let me do it," she said, taking the bottle from me.

"Oh, so you're all hot to drink champagne now?" I asked, watching her expertly remove the wiring and then apply herself to the cork.

"This is the least Sandstone can do," she said, and *POP!* the cork flew off the bottle, clanging ceremoniously into one of the copper pans hanging from the ceiling rack.

We toasted. Jorge said, "To family. That includes you, Dora."

I hoisted my glass and drank with the Mendezes. We killed that bottle, and drank another. Rosalyn smiled more in that hour than she had all summer. And Charlie acted like we'd just learned that our salaries were doubling. I was feeling way beyond tipsy on just two glasses, and was relieved when Jorge announced the party was over.

They all left together in the van. I stumbled home. My parents would smell the champagne on me, but I didn't care. I felt good. Better than I had in days, actually. It was peculiar, how bad news made me feel closer to these people.

I found myself fantasizing about our last day at the Brick. Jorge would fret the last prep. Charlie would set the last table. I'd butter the last piece of toast. Rosalyn would pour the last cup of coffee. And then we'd group hug, cry bittersweet tears and say things like, "I'll never work with a better bunch of people for the rest of my life."

Except Ramon and Raul would say it in Spanish. And I probably wouldn't understand it, but I'd smile and nod and say *"Sí, señor!"*

"Table of two," said Rosalyn, zipping into the kitchen, holding a few dirty plates. "They asked for you."

Sondra and Stanley again? No, they wouldn't be together after a breakup. I smiled, remembering how Stella spilled OJ on Sondra's lap. Then I recalled how decent Sondra was on our movie night. I owed her a free breakfast, which I was inclined to give. Since last week's news about the closing, I'd been giving customers (the nice ones) extra bacon and free juice refills. We all had. It was our little way to stick it to the man.

Only another week left at the Brick. Charlie and Rosalyn were talking a lot about returning to college next month. My senior year at Brownstone—along with SATs and college apps—was fast approaching.

My mother would be glad to know that, despite the anxiety of senior year, I was looking forward to it. The testing, the getting-into-college process. Although I wasn't exactly sure what I'd sorted out in my subconscious, something had changed. Mainly, my fear of the future had faded. And in its place? A feeling of expectation. I wasn't sure if I'd get into the college of my choice, whatever that was. I wasn't sure if I'd get decent scores. I wasn't even sure I still had a boyfriend. It bothered me less and less over the days and weeks. I'd stopped waiting for the phone to ring and praying for a postcard in the mailbox. I didn't know where the panic went, exactly. But it was gone, and good riddance. I wondered if this was the objectivity Dad spoke of, and if my achieving mental calm meant I had grown up a bit this summer.

I asked Rosalyn, "Two people? A guy and a girl?"

"I don't know," she said. "I barely looked. They waved at me and asked for you. So get out there."

I started to say something about asking a simple question and getting your ass chewed off, but Rosalyn was already off, preparing a plate for her tables. I watched her for a few seconds, her laser focus and the care she took in slicing a lemon wedge. I wondered what the legacy of my pseudofriendship with Rosalyn would be. I wanted to be a more responsible person. And for my dreams to be bigger than this

restaurant, this job, my school, my parents' expectations. No matter what, my dreams would probably
not be bigger than Brooklyn Heights, where you
could go on far-flung trips inside your head without
leaving the five-square-mile patch of pavement and
brownstone.

I wondered if Peaches's original owner ever read
my letter and if she liked it. I hoped she got it, and
that the letter gave her some comfort.

Rosalyn suddenly stopped slicing and glared at
me. "What're you looking at?" she asked.

"Nothing much!" I replied.

We laughed, together, as if we were *real* friends
and not just two women whose lives had overlapped
for a couple of months one summer. "Table for two,"
she reminded me. "Get your butt out there."

I got my butt out there.

Froze halfway to the table when I saw who it was.

Screams, girly, high-pitched and totally ridiculous, from me and Liza. Eli sat at the table, shaking
her head at our display.

Honestly, for a split second, I didn't recognize
Liza. She was tan, and her hair was a lighter blond
than usual. And she lost at least twenty pounds!
She'd always been sunny in demeanor and ample
in proportion. But now she was *skinny*, for the first
time in her life.

It happened to her, the over-the-summer physical

transformation every girl dreamed of. I'd been waiting for such an experience since I was twelve. I was still waiting.

"Holy crackers!" I said. "You left your belly in Bermuda!"

We grappled. The whole restaurant watched. I realized that the whole restaurant was already watching Liza in her smoking hotness.

Eli said, "It's impossible to be with her now."

"Ego?" I asked. Not our Liza.

"No! I mean logistically," said Eli. "Just walking down the street. Men clog the sidewalk to stare at her. Like they'd never seen blond hair before. I need sharper elbows to break through the crowd."

I giggled royally. It was like a warm bath, being with my best friends again. "You don't know how glad I am to see you guys."

Liza said, "We were concerned."

"About me?"

"You fell off a cliff," said Eli. "Metaphorically. No e-mails, IMs, text messages or calls."

"I needed to go off the grid for a while," I said.

"Two weeks???" said Liza. "That's an eternity."

Had I really been out of touch that long? Time flew when you weren't plugged in. "So you left paradise to make sure I was still alive?" I asked.

Liza flipped her now-platinum hair over her now-bony shoulder. "I was always going to come back to

Brooklyn for senior year. No way was some Irish son of a golf pro going to sway me. He turned into a bit of a groveling loser at the end anyway. I can do better. I blew off Stanley, too."

Eli and I made eye contact. She said, "A groveling loser? Blowing off boys left and right. Is this a taste of things to come?"

"What about you?" I asked Eli. "Glad to be home?"

"You have no idea," she said. "I left New York with tepid national pride. But being surrounded by rabidly anti-American Europeans for two months brought out this insane, jingoistic, patriotic fervor in me. I've decided to give up piano and go into politics. You're looking at our next class president."

"School government?" I asked, cringing. Nothing geekier than that.

"I like the ring of 'Madam President,'" said Eli, her black eyes shiny. "Don't you?"

It did have a nice ring to it.

Eli said, "So?"

"So?"

"Your story," prompted Eli.

"Nothing to tell," I said. More like, I just wasn't up for telling it. How could I explain to them that an accumulation of small events and one big shock had rearranged the functioning of my brain?

Eli said, "Nothing to tell? Do you expect me to believe that?"

I shrugged. "I'm not withholding. I made some friends; lost some friends. Had a couple jobs. Lost a couple jobs. Somewhere along the way, I stopped worrying about what was going to happen next. I just went along. I *got* along. By myself."

Liza and Eli nodded at me, as if they expected me to continue or elaborate. I wanted to. I would have. Except telling my friends the simple truth—that I'd grown up—would somehow erase the meaning of it.

"What about that cat you wrote to me about?" asked Eli.

"Well, she was sick when I took her in," I said, game face on. "She passed away peacefully. It's fine. I'm okay with it."

Liza said, "What about Noel?"

I said, "He's out there somewhere, I guess."

Eli asked, "He never called?"

"Nope," I said.

That shut them up. I hated to see them concerned on my behalf. "Look, I'm still on the clock. If the Brick members don't get their food, they start flipping tables, throwing knives. Hey, how did you guys get in here anyway? You're not members."

"Charlie," said Eli.

"Duh," I said. "Let me get you guys the biggest, greasiest free breakfast of your lives, and we can meet this afternoon when my shift is over."

Liza said, "I don't do big and greasy anymore."

Eli said, "Charlie and I are hooking up later."

She seemed torn. I didn't expect Eli to choose me over Charlie. And I wouldn't put her in that position. "Why don't we start with breakfast, and figure the rest out later. How about a stack of pancakes for you?" I said to Eli. To Liza: "And a fruit plate for my skinny friend?"

Eli said, "That sounds perfect."

Liza said, "You look different, too, Dora."

I scribbled on my pad. "How so? Please say bigger boobs."

"Older," said Liza.

"Wiser," said Eli.

22

Friday. My day off. Liza, Eli and I had plans to go to the floating pool. All summer, I cursed them for leaving me. But now that they were back, I was dragging my feet about spending time with them. Maybe "alone" had become my default preference.

Or, hopefully, I was just out of practice at being around my crew, and needed to push myself to get back in the swing, as it were, of our threesome. Eli and Liza were supposed to pick me up at my stoop in a few. I dressed quickly in my bikini and flip-flops, packed my beach bag and headed downstairs.

Mom and Dad were at the dining room table with, shockers, mugs of coffee. How they could drink scalding hot fluid when it was already over ninety (at ten in the morning) floored me. But Mom and Dad were hard-core java junkies. They would have their caffeine undiluted with ice, no matter what.

"I'm going," I said. "If anyone calls . . . forget it. No one's calling."

"Are you expecting to hear from someone?" asked Mom, her nose for news sniffing out the slightest hint of ambivalence.

"No," I said.

"Come home at a decent hour," said Dad. "If you want to kiss me good-bye before I go."

"Go where?" I asked.

They looked at me like I was deaf and dumb. Dumb, in the "stupid" sense. "I told you three times that I'm driving to Vermont to pick up Joya at camp."

"Right," I said.

"Are you okay?" asked Mom, her brows etched with concern.

"I'm fine," I said. "I'll be back for dinner, probably sooner."

Not wanting to get all into it with Mom—I could tell she was shifting into Inquisitor Mode—I rushed out of the apartment, ran down the stairs and out onto the stoop. I wasn't expecting to see many people out on Garden Place. We were a quiet block, not a main street. Random people hardly ever sat down on our stoops to rest or hang. In fact, when a stranger parked it on our stoop, it kind of freaked me out.

Hence, I wasn't happy to venture out of our brownstone and nearly collide with a homeless person on my stoop, sitting casually on the top step like he owned the place. The guy had long, shaggy hair, full beard and 'stache. He wore a grimy T-shirt that screamed "Bleach me!" His shorts were torn and ragged, like he'd been wearing them since the year Gimmel. And his sneakers! Simply vile. Like they'd crawled onto his feet and decided to feed off them. Next to him, a decrepit backpack. Probably contained everything he owned.

I closed the door behind me, my temper flaring at his impertinence in camping out on our stoop. But then the liberal sympathies kicked in. He probably just wanted to rest for a second. He had a hard life and didn't need some child of privilege telling him to get lost. From the back, he seemed pretty young, too. He'd probably suffered every day of his short life. Poor bastard.

He turned around at the sound of the door closing behind me.

The homeless guy looked oddly familiar.

"Dora!" he boomed. "Nice bikini."

He knew my name? "And you are?"

Then he laughed. Seeing my confusion, he said, "You're not serious."

"Oh. My. God," I breathed. "Noel? What *happened* to you? I heard you were chased by a bear. But I didn't realize you turned into one!"

He stood up, and came at me like a furry animal. I couldn't help stepping backward, and then remembered this hairy creature was my boyfriend (?).

I opened my arms to him and he slipped between them. He encircled my waist and lifted me high enough to kiss him.

Up close (thank GOD), he smelled fine. Good, actually. I realized the grime on his clothes was a clean filth. The ground-in variety that housewives complain about on TV commercials.

His beard scratched my cheeks. I'd never kissed a man with facial hair. And, had to say, I didn't especially like it.

The kiss, on the other hand—that I liked.

He lowered me, and my flip-flops touched the stoop. I opened my eyes and stared into his. They hadn't changed, the roiling, intense gray-blue that I'd taken long, luxurious swims in many, many times. He looked at me now with a pure heart, unvarnished affection, a natural love.

I said, "I hate you!"

"What?"

"You didn't call; you didn't write," I said, sounding like a Jewish mother. "I thought you were dead! Picked apart by turkey vultures in the woods!"

He said, "You knew I was fine. You were checking in with my mother. I have to say, when Mom told me you called, I was kind of shocked."

"I had to!" I said. "I was going crazy, Noel."

"I did call you," he said. "You weren't home, and you didn't pick up your cell."

That was true.

"Why didn't you keep trying?" I had to know. And then my weeks of missing him, worrying about him, worrying about us, hit me full force. I started babbling and crying. "I thought you forgot about me, or that you stopped caring about me. You sent a postcard to Stanley. You checked in with your mother. But you blew me off. And I was all alone here, Noel. And some pretty weird shit went down with people at my jobs, and I adopted a cat that I fell in love with. Absolute devotional worship, and then she died on top of my blue J.Crew cashmere sweater. I needed you, and then I decided I didn't need anyone, and fuck all of those people. Until I realized I do need people. Basically, I've been holding my breath to see you and touch you for two months, and now that you're here, I'm not sure how I feel. And your beard is totally not working for me."

Noel listened. He was an excellent listener. He waited for me to draw breath, and then he said, "Did you honestly believe that my feelings for you had changed, or were you just annoyed that I didn't try harder to reach you?"

I said, "*Just* annoyed? How about *furiously* annoyed. The mountaintop of annoyed."

He nodded, got it. "Besides that, did you really doubt me?"

I hadn't. Not a hundred percent anyway. But his

lack of contact was disconcerting. The silence created the space in my head for fantasies about Zack, but my loyalty to Noel kept me from going there, even when I had the opening.

I said, "You could have written to me. Just once. And then I'd've been okay."

Noel said, "I have something to show you."

He sat back down on the stoop and opened up the backpack. I sat next to him and couldn't help putting an arm around his shoulder and my hand on his knee. I had to touch him. I could have sooner cut off my own hand than removed it from his leg.

He withdrew a notebook. Spiral, blue. "I started writing a letter to you on my first night in the woods," he said, looking me in the eye. "I was scared, I admit. It was creepy out there, even with Dad. More so with Dad. The two of us barely knew each other, and we were alone with five million bugs."

"I bet you guys know each other now," I said.

"We know each other better," said Noel, nodding. "We know ourselves better, too."

So it'd been a big summer for him, too. I got the immediate impression that our time apart, and whatever emotional changes we'd each sustained, wouldn't drive us apart. It'd make us closer. Breathing that in, I watched my shaggy boyfriend open his notebook and turn to the first page. He seemed thinner, too, around the cheek and jaw. His neck and shoulders were ropy and tight. I'd bet his body had changed.

I couldn't wait to see him naked.

He said, "This is the letter."

I glanced at the page. It said, "Dear Dora" on the top, followed by handwritten text until the bottom. Noel turned the page. More writing on both sides of the notebook spread. He turned another page, and another. Each full of single-spaced handwriting. Occasionally, he took a break from text to include the drawing of an animal, leaf, bug or doodles. Otherwise, he'd filled page after page with words and sentences, all of them written to me.

"It started out as a letter to you, and then it just kept going and going," he said. "I didn't want to send it until it was finished, but I kept having more things to say. And then the letter turned into an epic, and I needed to have it for company." He handed over the notebook. "Don't read it now. Later."

I gladly took it. "I was with you on the mountain," I said.

"Every minute of every day," he said.

"I didn't feel that way about you here in Brooklyn."

He seemed sad about that. "I'm here now."

I leaned into him, and we kissed again. This wasn't a "hello" or a "welcome home." It was like zooming back in time, to how we kissed before he left, and then zipping into the future, to the future of Noel and me, not only as boyfriend/girlfriend, but as linked souls, destined to be part of each other's lives this time around, and in future lives, too, if you believed in reincarnation, which I wasn't sure I did, but wasn't ruling out as a possibility.

When we finally parted, I said, "You will shave?"

"You don't like it?" he asked, rubbing his facial growth against my cheek.

"Do I have to say it a third time?"

"Tell me about this cat," he said. "I bet you liked its facial hair."

I laughed. "Hers was soft."

"Mine's soft," said Noel, rubbing his beard.

"Like steel wool," I said.

"Come on, Dora," he said, rubbing the scruff against my cheek again. "You know you can get used to just about anything."

"Hey! You two on the stoop! Break it up!" A voice called from the top of the block.

We looked toward the sound. It was Eli, Liza at her side.

Noel said, "Is that . . . *Liza*?"

"Tongue back in mouth," I said to him. "She lost a little weight."

"A *little*?" he asked. "Stanley is going to have a heart attack when he sees her."

I let that one go. "Come swimming with us. We're going to the floating pool."

"You're leaving?" he asked. "But. But. I'm *here* now."

"And so are they," I said of my lifelong buds. "You're not going to ask me to make a choice between my boyfriend and my best friends, are you?"

"Yes," he said.

"Guys with beards don't sulk," I said.

"If I agree to go swimming," he said, "you have to let me keep the beard."

"Fine," I said, already plotting to go back on my word. "I look forward to seeing you with your shirt off."

"You can see me with my pants off, too, if you blow off Eli and Liza and come over to my place."

"I'm reading your letter first," I said. "I mean, before we even think about doing any of *that*."

"*What?*" he said. "It'll take hours to read the letter! And then we'll have to talk about it for hours. I've been thinking about *that* for months!"

At the bottom of the stoop, Eli said, "What's *that*?"

"Nothing," I said.

"Oh," said Eli. "*That.*"

"So, we're off," I said. "Noel's coming, too."

Liza's eyes bugged. "Noel? I didn't recognize you."

Eli said, "You thought Dora was making out with some random hairy person?"

"Yes?" said Liza.

"That's reassuring," said Noel. "It's a good thing I'm back, just to keep an eye on you."

I liked the sound of that. "Keep both of them on me," I suggested.

The four of us walked down Joralemon Street to the floating pool, docked in Brooklyn for only one more week. Rumor had it that the pool was moving to a site in the Bronx next summer.

We walked and talked. Eli and Liza commented on Noel's grizzly new look. Liza suggested that the picky pool staff might have to hose him down before they let him swim with people. I laughed along, felt happy to the core. It occurred to me that one hallmark of growing up was acknowledging the transience, and the permanence, of life. People, places, pets would flow in and out of my life. That said, I also believed that some things had to be constant. Like my family. The pavement beneath my flip-flops. The highway overpass above my head. The fixtures in my life were with me now as we walked in a tight group toward the water. No matter how much we all changed, or how profoundly our relationships changed, Eli, Liza, Noel and I would always have this moment of closeness. The memory was permanent. And that was something to be grateful for, regardless of what the future would bring.

23

I let her hug me. But when Joya tried to give me a sloppy wet kiss on the cheek, I drew the line.

"That's enough," I said, peeling her arms away from my neck.

"I missed you," said my kid sister.

I hadn't seen her in eight weeks. She hadn't grown much physically. She'd probably always be a shrimp, like Mom, but an achingly adorable one. Her usual pixie-cut brown hair was closing in on her shoulders. Anyone else, an unstructured two months of grow-out would be disastrous. On Joya, it looked smashing. The extra length around her face made her giraffe eyes seem even more enormous. Her shell-pink lips looked great with the sun-kissed cheeks.

Joya could roll around in a mud puddle and come out smelling like a fresh-cut rose.

Could make a person sick.

She asked, "Did you miss me, too?"

I grimaced. Did she have to make me say it? "The house was peaceful and clean without you," I said.

"So you did miss me!" she sang, and hurled herself at me again. "I made you a painting, Dora, inspired by your aura."

Oh, jeez, not the aura crap again. Joya claimed to be able to see the colored glow that radiated from a person's skin. Blue meant mellow, purple meant mad. Red meant sad. Yellow glad. Or not. I never paid attention when she rambled about it. I didn't doubt that Joya had aural visions. I doubted that she was sane. But whatever. I'd grown accustomed to her nutty babble.

After unloading, Mom and Dad went to park the car, leaving me and Joya alone for our reunion.

"It's in here," she said, placing a hand on a leather-bound portfolio of her drawings and painting.

"Are you going to show it to me, or what?" I asked.

"Do you really want to see it?" Joya's eyes beamed.

Did she have to be so damn needy? "Three, two . . ."

"Okay, let me find it."

She unzipped the portfolio and started flipping through page after page of drawings of all sizes. Then she stopped at a painting of a girl.

Clearly me. The angles of my face, the bangs, the sweep of thick hair and my swanlike neck. Joya had used pastels for the outlines, and watercolors for shading and detail. All in bright colors. Not a whisper of black on the entire portrait. And none of the colors she chose—purples, reds, blues—were found naturally on my body. I was a hazel-, honey-hued person. But Joya, apparently, saw me differently. Vividly. If a million people were to draw my picture, only Joya would have represented me this way, with electric blue, a purple mist and streaks of red.

The effect? Dazzling. I looked sort of lost, cynical, optimistic and a little bit angry. Despite our being three hundred miles apart, Joya had accurately captured my mood this summer, and put it on record beautifully. Hand to God, I'd have paid money to buy this painting. Theoretically. It occurred to me, in a real sense, that Joya's incessant drawing, since she was old enough to fist a crayon, might lead her somewhere. Like into the future. Joya was fourteen years old, and she was already an artist.

She watched me take it in. "Do you like it? Say you like it. Even if you hate it, say you love it. Don't hurt my feelings. If you hurt my feelings, I'm going to have to tell Mom and Dad."

An artist, yes, but still a huge pain in the arse.

"I love it, of course," I said. "It's the best thing you've ever done. I'm insanely jealous of your talent, even more than I was before. The portrait. It's exactly me. You nailed it. And you can stop jumping up and down now, or I'm going to smack you."

"I did a portrait of Ben, too. Want to see it?"

"Where the hell are Mom and Dad? They've been gone for half an hour already." Our parking garage was only three blocks away.

But Joya wasn't listening. She was flipping through sheets of paper and stretched canvas, describing her "process" for each one.

Thank GOD Mom and Dad finally returned. "Where have you been?" I asked.

"We parked the car," said Dad.

"In Calcutta?" I asked.

Mom said, "We also had an errand to run."

She gestured to the medium-sized cardboard box that Dad had just put on the table.

"Your mother and I have been talking," he said.

Never a good opener for a conversation. Usually, their "talks" resulted in the sudden, unwelcome decrease in TV or IM hours. Even Joya braced for the bad news.

I said, "She just got back from camp, for God's sake. Can't Joya relax for five minutes before you start in with the restrictions?"

Dad said, "I'm impressed by your protective impulse, Dora."

"Just looking out for Joya's well-being."

Mom said, "Without a single thought to your own interests."

"I learned how to be unselfish this summer," I assured Mom. "Read all about it in my college application essays."

That made Mom crack a reluctant smile. "Your father and I have been talking. . . ."

". . . And we've decided," continued Dad, "that we may have made a mistake in our duty as parents."

"A mistake?" I asked. "Meaning, one single, solitary mistake?"

"That's right," said Mom. "Your father and I are man enough to admit when we're wrong, and we're woman enough to try to fix it."

Joya said, "You haven't done anything wrong. You're great parents."

I said, "I'm ready to accept a steep increase in allowance."

Dad said, "In the box."

"You put twenties in there?" I asked. "It's kind of big, but whatever."

Joya said, "Can I open it?"

"Someone better," said Dad. "Or we might have a situation on our hands."

That was when the box started moving. And mewing.

Joya squealed and launched herself at it, flinging open the cardboard folds, peering inside.

Joya started jumping up and down again, clapping her hands. Two tiny heads popped out of the box. Four tiny paws clung to the edge. One of the kittens—black, with huge green eyes—looked right at me and let out a plaintive *meow*, as if it were saying, loud and proud, "What are YOU looking at?"

I laughed, and picked it—him? ahh, *her*—up. She was lighter than air. Her little claws hooked into my shirt, and when I tried to lift her away, she hung on, as if for dear life.

It amazed me how quickly you could fall madly, deeply in love.

The other kitten was white with blue eyes. A little fluff ball, perfect for Joya, who immediately claimed the marshmallow kitten, just as I'd been drawn instantly to the black one.

Mom said, "You approve?"

I said, "Thank you. Really, so much."

Dad said, "Do we need to tell you who helped us adopt the kittens?"

"No," I said.

"He was very nice," said Mom. "And he sent his best."

"He sure did," I said, snuggling my own kitten, who I'd cherish and love and cuddle every day for the rest of her life, unless I died first, in which case I'd have her buried with me, like King Tut.

"Better than a college application essay?" asked Dad.

"Better than college," I said.

Mom frowned and said, "But you are going to college."

"Yes, Mom," I replied. "And I'm taking her with me."

About the Author

Valerie Frankel is the author of thirteen previous novels, including *I Take This Man*, *The Accidental Virgin*, *The Girlfriend Curse*, *Hex and the Single Girl* and *Fringe Girl*. She writes often for magazines, including *Self*, *Glamour*, *Marie Claire* and *Allure*. When not working, Val plays Snood, blogs, jogs and takes amateur-quality digital portraits. She lives in Brooklyn Heights with her husband, two daughters and three cats. All of them are extremely photogenic. Go to www.valeriefrankel.com and see for yourself.